what the
heart
remembers

THE MEMORY HOUSE SERIES, BOOK THREE

BETTE LEE CROSBY

WHAT THE HEART REMEMBERS
Memory House Series, Book Three

Copyright © 2015 by Bette Lee Crosby

Cover design: damonza.com
Formatting by Author E.M.S.
Editor: Ekta Garg

ISBN-13: 978-0-9969214-0-4

BENT PINE PUBLISHING
Port Saint Lucie, FL

Published in the United States of America

For…

Jan Stacy Albritton

My Sweet Southern Sister

what the
heart
remembers

OPHELIA BROWNE

They say with age comes wisdom, but I'm not so certain that's true. By now I should have learned to temper my expectations, but I haven't.

I am in my ninety-first year of life, which is somewhat of a miracle. Women in the Browne family do not live long lives; it's a proven fact. For as far back as anyone remembers there has been only one cousin who made it to ninety-one, but she's three times removed and hardly worth a mention.

The truth is I expected to be long gone by now, but here I am. Alive and well. I've tried to adjust my expectations and take each day as it comes, but this is not an easy thing to do. Expectations are a way of life. Sadly enough, they are also what cause more heartache than anything else. I spent most of my ninetieth year waiting to die. Now I'm wishing I had that year back. Instead of worrying about dying, I'd be celebrating the fact that I'm still living.

The problem with expectations is that if you imagine something will be one way and it turns out differently, you're disappointed. It doesn't matter if the way it turns out is better, the simple fact is it's not what you expected.

When I left Memory House, I expected to leave other people's memories behind. I figured giving Annie the house meant all the magic would go with it, but I was wrong. Annie has her own kind of magic. It's different than mine, but in the years to come it will serve her well.

As for me, I still pick up the memories of other people. In the watch Sam carries I can picture the face of his daddy and the roughness of his callused hands. If I touch my fingers to the Rockettes picture hanging on Lillian's living room wall, my heart starts to race. I feel the anger she felt when she was moved to the end of the line. I see the pout of her mouth and hear her grumble, "This isn't fair!"

But those are simple memories. Clear cut. Over and done with. The saddest memories are those that won't let go. The kind Annie's friend Maxine carries around day and night. They're like a cloak tied tight around her shoulders. Even when she's deep in conversation or laughing out loud, I can see those memories poking a heartless finger into her brain. After all these many years, I've seen enough of other people's memories to know happy from sad. Max thinks those memories are happy, but they're not. Handsome men with flashy smiles blind a girl to the truth, and that's what has happened to her.

If she doesn't find a way to rid herself of those memories, she's in for a sorry life. And it's all because of her expectations.

December 31, 2014

The French claim the start of each year brings a renewal of dreams that have been set aside or forgotten. Max Martinelli hopes this is true. Three years ago she left Paris and returned to America. With less than two months to go until she received her accreditation as an architect, how could she not?

Back then it all seemed so simple. She would return and Julien Marceau would follow a month or two later. It was as certain as the rising of the sun or the setting of the moon. It was a plan sealed with a kiss that even now lingers on her lips. At night when she closes her eyes she can see his face hovering above hers and catch the citrusy scent of his cologne. But when she wakes he is gone. Somehow something went wrong, but what it was Max can't say.

MAX PULLS A BOTTLE OF CHILLED champagne from the car, trots up the walkway and taps the brass knocker. There are times when she visits Annie Doyle and doesn't bother to knock; she simply pushes the door open and calls out. But with Oliver working at home, she is more mindful of their privacy.

When Annie opens the door and sees Max, she pulls her into a warm embrace.

"Ooh, it's so good to see you," she says.

"I hope you didn't think I'd let this day go by without wishing you and Oliver a happy New Year," Max replies.

"No, but I thought you were going to a party at…"

"I am." Max twirls around. The side of her hair is pulled into a rhinestone clip, and beneath her coat there is the shimmer of a silvery blue satin. "See, no jeans!"

Annie gives a nod of approval. "You look fabulous," she says, and it brings a smile to Max's face.

"Before I go I figured we could have our own little celebration." She hands Annie the bottle of champagne then follows her back into the house.

As they pass through the hallway, Annie catches a wintery scent coming from the new bowl of potpourri. She turns back to Max and says, "Don't tell me you're thinking of snow."

Max laughs. "I guess I was. I was remembering the New Year's Eve I spent in Paris. It snowed that evening, so Julien and I skipped going to a party and stayed in." She gives a soulful sigh. "We had a bottle of wine, some day-old cheese and half of a baguette, but it was the most wonderful New Year's ever."

Annie knows the thought circling Max's mind. It is one that has surfaced many times, one Annie fears because she has come to love Max.

"There's a time and place for everything," she says, trying to turn the thought away gently. "Yesterday was yesterday. What was wonderful then may not be as wonderful now."

"I suppose." Max shies away from the subject, but it doesn't leave her mind. It hasn't for almost three years. On occasion she can push thoughts of Julien to the side and focus on work. But the memory of him inevitably comes back, and she is left to probe her thoughts for the answer to that burning question: Why?

As Annie crosses into the kitchen, she calls for Oliver. He is working in his study, reviewing the cases that will come before him when he returns to the courtroom in just seven short days.

When he enters the room, his walk is slower than it used to be. He has a slight limp; hardly noticeable, but Annie sees it. Since the accident, she takes nothing for granted. She watches over his every move the way a toddler's mother watches over her only child.

Oliver sees Max and smiles. "Happy new year," he says and pulls her into a warm hug. His arms and back have grown strong. There is little evidence of the damage that was done.

"You're looking good," Max tells him.

"I'm feeling great," Oliver replies. "Anxious to get back to work."

"Max brought champagne," Annie says and hands him the bottle.

As they talk he twists open the wire on the champagne bottle then pops the cork. He pours the bubbly wine into two flutes then takes a third and fills it with ginger ale.

"So," he says with a grin, "shall we celebrate the end of this year or the start of the new one?"

Annie and Max answer simultaneously. It is as if a single thought passes from one to another.

"The start of a new one," they both say, and then they laugh.

They are alike in so many ways it is little wonder they have become the best of friends. Their friendship is less than a year old, yet it has been this way from the start. Ophelia claims it is because of their unique abilities to lift the layers of reality and see what is beneath.

Oliver has no explanation; he simply accepts it for what it is.

He lifts his glass and makes a toast. "To the new year and the blessings it will bring." He glances at Annie. The swell of her tummy is only beginning to show, but the glow on her face is unmistakable.

She returns his smile and lifts the glass to her lips. She sips the ginger ale as if it were champagne. "And to finding a friend like Max," she adds.

"That goes both ways," Max echoes and raises her glass.

"Tough as this past year has been, I'm very thankful I had you beside me," Annie says. "You were there when I needed a shoulder to lean on, and that's something I'll never forget."

"And I'm thankful for the channeling tea you gave me," Max replies. "I've gotten three new clients since I began drinking it."

Annie is tempted to once again say the tea is nothing more than an herbal mix to promote focus and serenity, but she knows Max is happier believing in the magic of it.

"Well, then," she says, "we all have something to celebrate." As the three of them come together, there is again the clink of glass against glass.

Oliver glances at the champagne in his hand and then looks back to Annie. "When it comes to being thankful, I have both of you ladies beat by a mile." He tries to make his words sound light, playful almost, but the weight of this thought is visible in his expression.

"Are you trying to steal the show?" Max quips.

"No." He smiles. "I'm simply telling it like it is."

The smile on his face fades, and a look of contemplation sweeps across his brow. When he starts to speak, his voice falters as some of the memories come into focus. They bring both joy and sorrow.

"There was a time," he says solemnly, "when I laughed at the way you two found meaning in things that to me were simply things: a bicycle, a book, even the walls of a room. The thought that a memory could move beyond the person it belonged to or be left behind in an inanimate object seemed almost ludicrous."

Oliver sets his glass on the counter and crosses to where Annie stands. He wraps his arm around her waist, draws her closer, then looks at Max.

"I still don't understand it, but I've come to accept that you, Ophelia and Annie have some deal with the universe that's beyond my comprehension."

Max arches an eyebrow. "Meaning what?"

"I can't give you an explanation," Oliver says. "I only wish…"

There is a moment of hesitation; he lowers his eyes, and it is as if he is searching for his lost memories in the bubbles of champagne.

"I wish I could remember everything, but I can't," he says. "The days I spent in a coma are still a gigantic black hole. I remember seeing myself in the bed, but at the time I was somebody else. Who, I don't know. There seemed to be no night or day, no measure of time. I knew nothing of what came before or would come after. I was in one place and the man in the bed was in another. It was as if I was a balloon floating free with no string connecting me to him."

He hesitates again, and for a long moment there is only silence. He lifts the glass of champagne and drains it.

"When I heard Annie reading from my dad's book, I started to remember. The words didn't make any sense, but in between the words there were memories. Memories of Dad handing me the book; memories of Annie standing on my doorstep with a wide-eyed grin. Little by little I started to realize who was lying in that bed. Then I heard voices. A lot of voices. Louder than anything else, I heard Annie calling for me to wake up."

He stops and takes a deep breath, one that rattles through his chest and returns as a weary sigh.

"I still don't remember everything, but Annie was there and she remembers for me."

His eyes begin to water as he turns to her. His voice is weighted and crackles with emotion.

"Without your faith and persistence, I might not be here to celebrate the new year."

For a moment Max is speechless.

"Is that true?" she finally asks. "You really think you might not have found your way back if not for—"

He nods. "I'm fairly certain of it."

"Wow," she says. "I never thought I'd hear you say you believe—"

"I'm not saying what I do or don't believe," Oliver cuts in before she can finish the thought. "After all, I'm a judge. I've spent most of my life making decisions based on fact. But I've come to accept there are certain realities that have no logical explanation..."

As he continues to speak Max's mind wanders, and she drifts back to that last goodbye when Julien held her in his arms and promised—

"Are you all right?" Annie interrupts her reverie.

"All right?" Max sputters. "Of course I'm all right. I was just thinking I'd better get going or the party will be over by the time I get there."

She downs the last of her champagne, sets the glass on the counter and reaches for her coat.

Annie walks with her to the door. "We'll see you tomorrow, won't we?"

"Of course," Max answers. "I'm looking forward to it."

As she watches Max disappear down the walkway, Annie calls out, "Drive safely."

This is what Annie now says to all those she loves. After the accident that nearly took Oliver's life, a fear has settled in her heart. It is one that has already grown roots and will never leave. Statistics say that only one person in ten thousand motorists will be killed in an automobile collision, but still she worries. She worries that the one person could be someone she loves.

THE PARTY

The party is at LuAnn Barkley's apartment in downtown Richmond. It is well over an hour from Wyattsville but Max hasn't seen these friends since graduation, so she's opted to make the drive. By the time she arrives, the festivities are in full swing. Silver and black balloons bobble overhead, and the stereo is turned up so loud the walls vibrate.

Before Max has time to shed her coat, Brianna Mosley spots her and rushes over. She gives an air kiss and gushes that it's been ages since they've seen one another.

"Where on earth have you been keeping yourself?" Brianna asks.

"Mostly working," Max answers.

Brianna rolls her eyes. "Working?"

Max nods with a feigned smile. "I've been doing some relatively small redesign projects; nothing big, but I'm getting my name out there."

Although Max is decked out in party gear she still has the big black leather satchel she carries every day slung over her shoulder. She reaches into it, pulls out a business card and hands it to Brianna.

Brianna eyes the card. "You have your own firm! Awesome," she says, sounding impressed. "How many employees?"

"Just me," Max replies. "I work out of my apartment." She spots the way Brianna is looking down her nose at such a thought and adds, "But once I have a few more clients, I plan on setting up an office."

"You need one now," Brianna says. "If you had a real office, clients would take you seriously. You'd get more work and better fees. You know what they say, it's the sizzle that sells." She tilts her head back and laughs.

"Maybe in a year or two," Max says with a sigh. "When I can afford it."

Again Brianna rolls her eyes. She glances across her shoulder then leans closer and in a hushed voice whispers, "The secret to success is to marry money. Wayne set me up in a studio big enough for exhibitions." She gives a self-satisfied grin then adds, "If you want I can have him introduce you to some of his friends."

"No thanks," Max replies.

She now remembers why she's avoided getting together with Brianna for the past few years. Across the room she spots a familiar figure.

"Excuse me," she says, "I've got to say hi to Jeff. I haven't seen him since—"

"Suit yourself," Brianna cuts her off, "but if you change your mind and want to meet a man who can set you up in the kind of office you need, call me."

Max promises to do just that, then pulls away and inches across the room. She stops to chat with several others before she finally reaches the far side.

Jeff is standing beside a woman he introduces as his wife. He then produces a wallet filled with pictures of a round-faced baby with no hair.

"This is our Kylie," he says proudly. "Isn't she adorable?"

Max smiles and gives a nod of agreement. After she has seen a dozen pictures of the bald baby, she moves on.

This is how the evening goes. Max circles the room greeting friends she has long ago lost touch with and chatting about things that somehow seem of little interest. Perhaps if her thoughts were not elsewhere...perhaps if she was not thinking back on what Oliver said...maybe these people talking about their lives would be of greater interest.

Max finds it almost impossible to generate enough enthusiasm to speak of her own life. She is at a loss for what to say. It would be of little interest to hear that she has a small practice with a handful of random clients or that her apartment is barely large enough to hold the clutter of drawings, a drafting table and a bed, a single at that.

Standing in the center of the crowded room, she feels terribly alone. It is as if she has stumbled into a room filled with strangers.

This isn't what Max expected. These people were her friends. She'd partied with them all through school. They guzzled beer together and pooled resources to buy a pizza. They sat alongside one another and commiserated on student loans. *Friends forever,* they'd said. But in three short years they morphed into a group of strangers; people with successful businesses, happy marriages and babies. They moved on while she got stuck in a holding pattern, a pattern that kept circling back to ask, "Why?"

At eleven forty-five LuAnn snaps on the television and announces, "It's almost time!" She looks around the room to make certain everyone is equipped with paper hats and noisemakers, then hurries over and hands Max a sequined band with a gaudy yellow feather.

"Now you need a noisemaker," she says.

"No, no, I'm okay," Max protests, but it does no good.

LuAnn rushes off, and moments later she is back with a paper horn. "Here you go," she says then disappears again.

At eleven fifty-nine the group clusters around the television, counting along as the crystal ball descends into 2015. They are as one voice echoing, "Nine, eight, seven, six..." When the announcer shouts "Happy New Year!" LuAnn tosses a handful of confetti into the air. Husbands bend and kiss their wives full on the mouth. Many whisper something special to their loved one; then they turn to friends and share cheek-grazing kisses.

The longing Max has carried for so long swells and becomes a hardened lump in her throat. In a voice that is dry and scratchy, she returns the greeting that others give her. "Happy New Year," she says, but the truth is it's not at all happy.

It is barely twelve-fifteen when Max goes to LuAnn and thanks her for the invitation. "I've got a bit of a drive," she offers as an excuse for leaving so early. She then makes her way to the door and slips out almost unnoticed.

Brianna catches her eye as Max pulls on her coat. She holds her hand to the side of her face with her pinky and thumb extended as she mouths the words, *Call me if you change your mind.*

Max returns the smile and nods. She knows, just as Brianna probably knows, that such a call will never happen.

Although Julien Marceau is not in the room this night, he is at the forefront of Max's mind. She wonders where he is and if perchance he also remembers the New Year's Eve they spent together.

AS MAX DRIVES HOME, SHE replays Oliver's words. *Without you I would not be here to celebrate the new year...what I don't remember, Annie remembers for me.* The words run through her thoughts over and over until she gives them room to grow. Room to become more than just words. Room to become a sorrowful wish. As she drives through the dark of night leaving one year behind and moving into the new one she wonders: what if Julien suffered a fate such as Oliver's? What if he is left with no memory of her, no memory of anything?

It's possible, she tells herself. At the back of her mind the small voice of reason argues, *Possible maybe, but not probable.* She pushes back such a thought and moves on to a deeper level of wondering.

As she slides into her pajamas she imagines Julien walking through the catacomb of tunnels that connect one metro station to another. The tunnels are endless and nearly deserted in the wee hours of the morning. He could have been mugged or grown dizzy and toppled into the path of an oncoming train. No one would know to contact her. No one would know where to call.

This has been a long day. Too long. She climbs into bed and tugs the blanket up around her shoulders. As her eyelids flutter shut she pictures the Honda motorcycle Julien rode. It was way too small. Not safe. Anything could send it flying across a busy intersection: a loose cobblestone, a crevice in the roadway…

She hears a familiar sound and listens. It is the wonk-wonk of a police car. Behind it there is the roar of motorcycles and voices chanting. She is back in Paris. It is a small room, barely wide enough to squeeze past the chair and push open the window. It has a cook stove that at times refuses to work and a crack in the wall where the icy cold of winter slides through.

Julien moves past her and throws open the window. The voices are louder now, angrier. He waves to the crowd in the street, shouts something, then pulls his jacket from the hook and heads for the door.

"Don't go," she says.

He turns back and flashes a smile. "Don't go? Haven't you always known I would go?"

Before she can answer he is out the door.

She moves to the window and sees him dart from the

building. In what seems less than a heartbeat, he is swallowed up by the throng of protestors.

She stands and watches until the parade of people rounds the corner and starts down the side street. Long after he is gone from sight, she can hear the heady sound of his laughter.

She steps back ready to pull the window shut, but there is a sudden burst of gunfire. The rat-a-tat-tat is followed by shouts and crying. She can no longer hear the lilt of his laughter. Leaning out beyond the ledge, she screams his name.

"Julien! Julien!"

MAX WAKES WITH A START and sits up. She is soaked through with perspiration but can still feel the chill that has settled in her bones.

Now more than ever she is convinced something has happened to Julien, something that kept him from coming to her.

January 1, 2015

It is New Year's Day, and everyone is gathering at Memory House. Ophelia comes with Lillian, Sam and Pauline, her new friends from Baylor Towers. They arrive in the Baylor limousine, which is how Ophelia now travels. There is no more driving, not after what happened.

Just the thought of Ophelia or one of her friends behind the wheel of a car gives Annie hives. Blisters rise up, and there is not a potion in the entire apothecary powerful enough to rid her of the itch. Knowing the Baylor car is on hand to take the group wherever they want to go gives Annie the peace of mind an expectant mother needs.

She is not due until the second week of May, but Annie has already felt the baby move. On quiet nights when she and Oliver lie side by side in bed, he places his hand on her stomach and swears he can tell the baby is a boy.

"The way that little rascal is moving around, it's got to be a boy," he says.

Ophelia, although she has never had any children of her own, claims the baby is a girl.

"I'm practiced in knowing what's beneath a person's skin," she says, adding that she's also got a woman's intuition.

"The child will be born with violet eyes and your gift of perception," she predicts. "Before the girl is twelve, she will be able to touch her hand to a memory and claim it as her own."

Annie turns away from such a thought because she is uncertain whether having this gift is what she wants for her child. It is a double-edged sword. True, the bicycle boy's memories are what led her to Oliver, but there are other memories, ones with anger and violence attached to them. Finding the memories left behind by other people is like opening Pandora's Box. There is simply no way of telling the good from the bad until you are holding it in your hand, and by then it is often too late.

Although she believes Ophelia's prediction will turn out to be nothing, Annie is taking no chances. On the back burner of the stove a huge pot simmers. It is the black-eyed peas that have soaked in water since yesterday. This morning she rinsed them for a third time then added chunks of bacon and onion. In the oven a ham drizzled with honey is browning. Annie knows the ham is what people will reach for first, but it is the peas that will bring good luck. Hopefully.

Today there will be eight at the table. Not family, but friends who are close as family. Ophelia will sit at the head of the table. It is where she sat for half a century, and Annie wants to hang on to the tradition. Oliver will sit at the other end. She has tactfully positioned Andrew Steen across the table from Max, close enough to chat but not close enough for their knees to bump up against each other. She hopes to avoid the testy innuendos that occurred last time.

Just as Annie is pulling the ham from the oven, the doorbell chimes. Andrew and Max arrive—not together but simultaneously.

When Oliver opens the door, Andrew steps back and motions for Max to enter. "Ladies first."

Max gives a tight-lipped smile. "Thanks."

With a quick greeting to the group that is already gathered she hurries by. "I've got to get this in the fridge," she says and holds up the bottle of champagne.

Andrew carries a pot of yellow chrysanthemums, but he is in no hurry. He sets the flowers on the coffee table and leans down to kiss Ophelia's cheek.

"You're looking well," he says then turns to greet the others.

It is easy to see why Oliver and Andrew were successful as law partners; they both have the same good-natured manner.

Oliver slings his arm across Andrew's shoulder. "So how's it going?"

"Good," Andrew answers. "This international product liability stuff is keeping me hopping. Winnie is working full time now."

Winnie is Andrew's law clerk, not a student but a woman in her early fifties. A woman who studied to become a lawyer, then settled into marriage and a family before she'd had time to take her final exams.

"Is she thinking of going for the bar?" Oliver asks.

Andrew laughs. "You know Winnie. One day she's dead set on getting her license, the next day she's off to do something with the grandchildren."

"That's Winnie," Oliver chuckles. Fond memories of the casual office environment he shared with Andrew cross his mind and linger for a moment.

"Give her a hug for me," he says.

When Max returns to the room, Andrew picks up the chrysanthemums and starts toward the kitchen. He passes her, smiles and gives a nod but says nothing. Not because he doesn't like Max; he just doesn't want an act of friendship to be mistaken for something more. Not after what she said at their last meeting.

IT IS A WHILE BEFORE Andrew returns to the living room, and when he finally does Annie is with him.

"Dinner is served," she says.

The group makes their way to the dining room and settles at the table. Once everyone is seated, Oliver says a prayer. He thanks the Lord for bringing them through the troubles of the past year and asks that He continue to do so in the year that lies ahead.

"Amen to that," Ophelia says and scoops a sizable portion of black-eyed peas onto her plate. "I was hoping you'd make this," she tells Annie. "A new year without black-eyed peas doesn't bode well."

One word leads to another, and before everyone has finished filling their plate a number of conversations zigzag across the table.

After hearing Ophelia's explanation that the black-eyed peas are rumored to bring good luck, Sam adds a second scoop to his plate.

"I could use some luck," he says mournfully. "This week I lost a dollar eighty-seven to Jack Sauer, and he's the worst pinochle player in the group."

Lillian laughs. "Jack's not the worst player, you are."

Sam gulps down a forkful of peas and replies, "That's about to change."

As the group settles into eating there is a lull in the conversation and Annie asks Max, "How was the party last night?"

She shrugs. "Okay, I guess."

"Okay doesn't sound like much of a party," Oliver says with a laugh. "Didn't you get to see your friends from college?"

Max nods. "Yes, I saw them but..."

She stops. This isn't what she intended to talk about today. The feeling of loneliness that took hold of her at the party is still heavy in her heart. She hoped to bury it, push it to the back of her mind and never think of it again, but that's impossible. The hurt is right there on the tip of her tongue, waiting to be told.

"But what?" Annie asks.

"They've changed," Max replies. "The things they talk about, the things they say…"

Andrew knows the feeling. Two years ago he left his class reunion after only an hour and hasn't been back.

"That happens," he says softly. "Everyone grows in a different way; maybe you've outgrown them."

"It's more like they've outgrown me," Max replies. Suddenly it is spilling out, one word after another. She speaks of all the friends who have married or moved on to successful careers. None of those people are the reason Max is lonely, but she lets herself believe they are.

"Brianna Mosley," she says angrily, "a girl who never did an honest day's work in her life, had the gall to tell me that if I didn't have an office, clients wouldn't take me seriously."

"That's true," Andrew says. He should know better. He should see the hurt tugging at Max's face and hear the bitterness of her words, but he doesn't.

"I don't know that I'd say they wouldn't take you seriously, but people are more respectful of a legitimate business location."

He continues, not noticing how Max's nose twitches side to side.

"Clients figure if you're working from home, you're freelancing. They see you as someone who's just looking to pick up some extra money, not really—"

"Would anyone like another slice of ham?" Annie cuts in. She has seen the look on Max's face and senses what is about to happen.

"I'll take one," Sam answers and passes his plate down.

Ophelia has also noticed Max's expression, and she jumps in to help Annie.

"I'll have another scoop of those black-eyed peas," she says. "Is that collard greens you've got mixed in with them?"

"Why, yes it is," Annie replies. "Mama used to say adding greens to the New Year's peas will bring money as well as luck." She leans over and covers Max's hand with her own. "I added the collard greens especially for you," she says affectionately.

Max gives a wan smile, and the moment of intensity passes without incident.

THE CONVERSATION MOVES TO OTHER things: football, the apothecary and news of the day. Max doesn't mention Julien; for now he is only in her thoughts.

After dinner she follows Annie into the kitchen and helps to clean up. As she stacks the dishes in the sink, Annie asks, "Do you want to talk?"

"Yes," Max answers, "but not tonight."

Annie doesn't push it. "Whenever you're ready," she replies then pulls Max into an embrace of friendship.

For the remainder of the night Max steers clear of Andrew. She doesn't look him in the eye, sit within speaking range or pass him going through the hallway.

Andrew unfortunately does not get the opportunity to give voice to what he had in mind. In his office there is a room that three years earlier was Oliver's office. It is still empty, and he was going to tell Max she is welcome to use it if she wants to.

MAX MARTINELLI

Sometimes it takes a jolt to make you wake up and see what you're doing to yourself. For the past three years I've been living a lie. It's one thing to lie to other people, but I've also been lying to myself. I say I'm over Julien, he's a thing of the past, but that's not true.

Instead of moving on, I'm stuck in a place where he's not part of my life but he's enough to keep me from having a life.

Last year I designed the reception area for a good-looking chiropractor who was just starting out. I could see he was flirting with me, but instead of enjoying the moment and allowing myself to like him I started comparing him with Julien. When you have an image of perfection fixed in your mind, it's impossible for anyone to measure up.

The problem is there's no ugliness tied to Julien. He was always carefree and full of fun. We almost never fought or got angry at one another; it was just this perfect relationship, and then nothing.

I know it sounds ridiculous to look back and wish we'd had arguments and bitterness, but without those things you have nothing to regret. You don't regret having a wonderful relationship; you just keep looking back and wishing you still had it. That's what I'm now doing.

If the relationship was wonderful for me, I would think it had to be wonderful for Julien also. That's why I don't understand him not getting in touch.

I've thought about it for so long my head is ready to split open. The only answer I've come up with is that something happened to him. Something that would cause him to forget me, maybe even forget everything he ever knew.

It happened to Oliver, so it's possible it could happen to Julien also. Okay, maybe it's a long shot, but I owe it to myself to find out for sure.

I don't want to spend the rest of my life wondering what would have happened if we had gotten back together. That's no way to live. When you come to a crossroad in life, you've got to take one pathway or the other. Just standing in the middle of the road means you've got nothing to look forward to because the only thing you can see is what's behind you.

Maybe I won't find Julien or find him married to some cute little French girl, but it's the chance I've got to take. This can turn out one of two ways. I can be reunited with the man I love and come home deliriously happy, or I can discover he's moved on and no longer wants me.

Either way, it's still better than not knowing.

THE DECISION

In the week following the New Year's Day dinner, Max finishes the design of a freestanding kiosk for the Gold & Glitter Shop. But as she sits in front of the computer pulling together a three-dimensional rendering, her mind is not on the project. Even as she blocks in the banner headline, she is thinking of Paris. She remembers walks along the Seine, a small bistro in Rue Cler and the feel of Julien's hand pressed to the small of her back.

At first the thought of returning to look for him seems ludicrous, but as the days pass it begins to grow on her. By the end of the week she is convinced that only an accident too horrible to imagine could have kept him from coming to her.

She remembers Oliver that first night in the hospital—a man who heard nothing, saw nothing and had no memory. Then the image takes on Julien's face. Max gasps. She has created this picture herself, and yet it shocks her.

*What if...*she wonders. What if such a fate befell Julien?

For two nights she finds sleep impossible to come by. The moment she closes her eyes he is there. Sometimes he lies beside her on the grassy lawns of the Tulleries; other times he walks the pathway alone, his face a blank canvas, his eyes vacant and unseeing. Both images are troubling, but the one where he is alone even more so because when it comes Max is again reminded of Oliver's words. *When I couldn't remember, Annie remembered for me.*

OVER THE PAST WEEK ANNIE has left three messages on the answering machine, but Max has yet to return the call. She knows Annie is concerned, but she is not ready to talk. A voice in the back of her mind keeps urging her to move on, to forget what was and turn her eyes to what could be. And there are times when she thinks the voice might be right.

She has enough money in her savings account to open a small office. She could reach out to her existing clients, ask for referrals, broaden her circle of friends, join a gym, meet new people. All of this seems possible until she closes her eyes and the image of Julien comes back.

After a week of wrestling with such thoughts, she finally returns Annie's call.

"I'm sorry," she says, "I've had a lot on my mind."

"No problem." Annie's reply is soft and mellow, like a pillow inviting you to rest your head. "I've created a new cinnamon ginger tea. If you have time, stop over and try it."

"Is now okay?" Max asks.

Minutes later she is out the door.

THERE IS SOMETHING ABOUT MEMORY House that makes a person feel welcome. This is how it has been for as far back as anyone can remember. Some believe it is because of the potpourri that sits in the entryway and gives off the scent of whatever a guest has in their thoughts; others claim it is the aroma of lavender that, even in the dead of winter, comes from the apothecary.

Max believes the magic of the house is hidden in the walls. How it got there or where it came from, she cannot say. She only knows that it is.

When she arrives Annie has already set out a plate of hazelnut cookies and a pot of the new cinnamon ginger tea. She hugs Max and says it is good to see her.

"It's good to be here," Max replies. Again she apologizes. "I'm sorry about not returning your call—"

Annie waves her off. "Don't give it a second thought. I understand you've been busy." She knows this isn't the real reason for Max not calling but hopes to smooth the pathway for her to say what is on her mind.

Today they sit at the kitchen table because it is far too cold for the back porch. It is barely three o'clock, and yet the sky is dark with heavy clouds and the threat of snow hanging in the air. For a long while they talk of inconsequential things: the Gold & Glitter kiosk, a new crochet pattern, the quilt shop sale.

By the time Max finds courage enough to speak her thoughts, the tea in her cup has grown cold. She takes one last sip then pushes the cup aside.

"I've finally decided to do something I should have done a long time ago."

Annie expects Max to say that at long last she is going to open her own office, but instead she says she is going to Paris in search of Julien.

"You're kidding!" Annie says.

Max shakes her head. "No, I'm not. I've given this a lot of thought, and until I know the truth—"

"It's been over three years!"

"I realize that, but maybe—"

"He hasn't even tried to get in touch with you!"

"That's true," Max replies sadly, "but if something happened—"

"What could possibly happen?" Annie counters. "Even if he lost your address, he could have found you on Facebook or even the damn yellow pages!"

"He's not on Facebook," Max says. "I've looked."

A roll of thunder sounds. It is near; not overhead, but near. Annie glances out the window, and the sky is black as night. This is not a good sign, but still she continues. "He's supposed to be an artist, isn't he? He must have some sort of business listing. Try LinkedIn, or Google him."

"I've done all that," Max replies wearily. "Several times." She says something more, but the thunder comes again and her words are lost beneath the sound of it.

"What was that?" Annie asks.

Max raises her voice to be heard.

"It's possible he's been in some sort of accident," she yells, "and has amnesia!"

The thunder falls silent, and Max's last word sounds loud as the bang of a kettledrum.

"Amnesia?" Annie stares at Max in wide-eyed disbelief. "Really?"

Max nods. "It's possible."

Before Annie can answer there is another boom of thunder; this one is directly overhead. It comes with such force it shakes the walls of the house. A second and third burst follow, both as powerful as the first. While the sound still hangs in the air, a streak of lightning cuts across the sky. Moments later the lights go out, and they are in total darkness.

"Stay there," Annie says. "I've got candles in the cupboard."

She pushes her chair back and feels her way towards the counter. In the pitch-black room it seems as though nothing is where it is supposed to be, and it is several minutes before she can light a candle and carry it to the table.

As she lowers herself into the chair, Annie sees the tears in

Max's eyes and remembers what hopelessness feels like. It's a pain that hollows out everything you've got inside. It leaves you feeling you are worthless, good for nothing and unlovable. She stretches her arm across the table and covers Max's hand with her own.

"You're the most beautiful person I know," she says tenderly. "I just don't want to see you get hurt."

"I know." Max gives a sad little smile. "But I've got to do this. Please understand."

"I can't say I understand," Annie replies, "but I'll be there for you no matter what. I just want you to think about it for a while; think about it and make certain it's what you *really* want to do."

"I will," Max sniffles. "I promise I will."

Annie believes this because it is what she wants to believe.

ANNIE

I wanted to tell Max she's making a mistake, a terrible mistake, but I couldn't do it. I love her too much. There's a big difference between giving someone helpful advice and squashing their dreams.

I know what she's going through because I've been there. It's the same way I felt when Michael Stavros walked out and left me. The problem with loving such a man is that you're blinded to everything but his smile. You can't see the arrogance of his soul or the selfishness of his actions. His beauty draws you in, and that's all you see. He whispers that he's the beginning and the end of it all, and you foolishly believe him.

Listening to the stories Max tells about Julien, he sounds exactly like Michael: a man who loves himself way more than he could ever love anyone else. A man such as that will never bring happiness. Heartache and misery, that's all he has to offer.

The problem is you can't see this until you muster up enough courage to walk away. When you finally turn your back on him he whines and cries about how much he loves you, but if you listen you're lost.

Nobody can save you from a love like this; you have to save yourself. The only way you'll ever be free is to walk away and not look back.

God knows if there were a way to make Max forget Julien, I'd do it. She's my best friend, and I don't want to see her get hurt. Tragic as this may be, there's nothing I can do.

She says she's going to go in search of him, and if she decides to actually go through with it I won't be able to stop her. Sure, I could badger her with the thousands of reasons for not doing it, but then she'd turn a deaf ear and stop talking to me. I don't want that to happen. I love her as much as I love Ophelia and Oliver, but I have to back off and trust she'll make the right decision.

That might sound easy but trust me, it's not. When you're afraid someone you love is going to be hurt, doing nothing is the hardest thing in the world.

THE COPPER KETTLE

In the weeks that follow there is no further discussion of Julien, not even a mention of his name. Max has three projects underway and the latest one, the addition of a second family room to Doctor Kelly's house, offers a myriad of challenges. Denise Kelly wants a wall of built-ins and an entertainment area large enough to accommodate a dozen friends. The doctor's only interest is in seeing the project does not exceed his $40,000 budget.

After three rounds of changes and design revisions, Max finally gets the construction estimate down to $42,000.

"I suppose I can live with that," Doctor Kelly says, and Denise smiles.

Max promises that once the project gets underway she will be available to answer questions and consult with the builder. As the doctor signs his initials to approve the plans, Denise gives Max a sly wink.

"You'll love working with Mark Treadway," she says. "He's tall, good looking and—"

The doctor is short and balding, so this is apparently a sore spot.

"Denise," he says sharply. "There's no need to—"

"Okay, okay." She shrugs and leaves off the part about Mark Treadway also having the kind of charm that can cause a woman to forget she's married.

When the doctor goes back to initialing the copies, Denise looks at Max and mouths the words *I'll tell you about him later.*

Max shakes her head and waves off such a thought. The truth is she's not interested in Mark Treadway. Right now the only thing she's interested in is finishing up the projects on her drawing board.

ON THE THIRD MONDAY OF March the countertop cosmetics display is delivered, and two weeks later the drawings for the Meyers' kitchen are finalized.

The following Tuesday Max suggests she and Annie have a girls' day out. They plan lunch at the Copper Kettle and a bit of shopping afterwards.

"It'll be good to see you," Annie says. "It's been too long."

Max has seen Annie only three times since January. She's stayed away because she can't trust herself to not talk about this. She can't be angry with Annie for not wanting her to go, but neither can she listen to all the reasons why she shouldn't be doing it. In a small corner of her mind Max wonders if maybe Annie isn't right, but when that thought comes she pushes it back and focuses on her memories of Julien. Some nights she falls asleep almost certain she will find him; other nights she sobs into her pillow daunted by the prospect of failure.

Now there is no longer time for procrastination. With only eight days remaining, she has to tell Annie about the plane ticket tucked in the top drawer of her bureau.

A half-hour before she is to head out the door, the telephone rings. Max picks it up; hopefully Annie is not going to cancel.

A male voice says, "Maxine?"

Not since Julien has anyone called her Maxine. Not even her father on the rare occasion when he visits. She answers tentatively, "Yes, this is Max."

"Mark Treadway here," he says.

It takes a moment before the name registers. "Oh, yes," she sputters, "you're Doctor Kelly's builder."

"Construction engineer," he says with a chuckle.

"Don't tell me you've already run into problems."

"No. We're not scheduled to start the job until late April, but Denise said I should give you a call. I thought perhaps we could get together for a drink, go over the plans, you know, kind of outline our expectations."

Max remembers the smile on Denise's face when she spoke of Mark.

"I'm sorry," she says, "but this isn't a good time. I'm leaving for Paris next week and have a really tight schedule right now."

"Oh." The sound of his disappointment is obvious. "Denise said you were available."

For consultation not recreation, Max thinks. "I can give you a call when I get back and maybe stop by your office; would that work?"

He hesitates then admits, "I don't have an office. I work from home or the job site. How about we meet at your office?"

Max laughs. "I don't have an office either. I work out of my house." For some odd reason saying this is not uncomfortable, and for once she doesn't feel embarrassed by not having an office.

They talk for a while longer, and Max promises to call when she gets back. She scribbles his number on a scrap of paper and tosses it into the kitchen catch-all drawer.

By the time she sits down to lunch with Annie, Mark Treadway has been long forgotten.

THE COPPER KETTLE IS A small restaurant and one of the few that serves a variety of teas as well as cocktails. They settle into a booth, and Annie orders a double spice chai. Max opts for a glass of burgundy. Today is a day of leisure; they are in no hurry to order lunch so they push the menus aside and talk. Mostly it is a conversation that meanders from one subject to another without ever skipping a beat.

"It's seems like it's been ages since we did this," Annie says.

Max laughs. "It has been ages since we treated ourselves to day out."

"The last time was..." Annie rubs her fingers across her forehead and pinches the top of her nose. She finally sighs. "Good grief, I can't even remember when the last time was."

"I think it was right after Ophelia moved to Baylor Towers."

"You're right!" Annie laughs. "I remember how worried I was about Ophelia, and then I met her friends at Baylor. I still wasn't happy about the move, but at least I wasn't worried anymore."

"Sometimes you've just got to trust that a person knows what's best for themselves," Max says.

Annie picks up the menu and is browsing the specials when she senses the thoughts circling through Max's mind.

"Don't tell me." She gives a weary sigh.

This is how their friendship has been from the very start. Both of them somehow know what the other is thinking. Ophelia claims if she didn't know differently she would swear they were twins born of the same egg. Annie laughs at such a thought, but she also has to admit that it is indeed strange.

"I thought you'd given up your thoughts of him," she says.

Max shakes her head. "No, but I had a couple of projects I had to finish. Two days ago I delivered the last one."

Annie already knows the answer, but still she asks the question. "So are you going over there to try and find him?"

They both know the "there" is Paris and the "him" is Julien.

Max nods. "I leave a week from tomorrow."

Annie lowers the menu and pushes it away; suddenly she has no appetite. "This is a mistake, Max. You know it is. Don't you think if he loved you—"

"Julien did love me, I know he did," Max replies. "What I don't know is what happened." It is too painful to look straight into Annie's eyes, so she looks down at the table focusing on a droplet of spilt wine. "Our relationship was something special. There's no way a man goes from a love like we had to...nothing." She hesitates then heaves a sigh that rattles through her chest and spills out with pieces of her heart stuck to it. "Unless..."

"Unless what?"

"Unless something happened to him."

Annie drops her forehead into the palm of her hand. "That's not logical. You know it's not logical. Why would you pin your hopes on a possibility that is—"

"It's better than not having any hope," Max cuts in. "Trying to understand the logic of things can keep a person from having hope." She tucks a finger under Annie's chin, lifts her face and looks into her eyes. "Logic would say a book of law couldn't possibly be the thing that would bring Oliver out of his coma, and yet..."

Annie's eyes grow tearful as she remembers.

"You believed in him enough to try," Max says, "and you were able to bring him back."

Annie gives a silent nod.

"Well, I believe in Julien enough to try. I believe if he was able to, he would have come to me."

"What if you find him and he doesn't want to remember you?"

"Then I'll come home and start my life over again. But at least I'll be able to stop wondering and looking back."

Annie has no answer for that.

OPHELIA

Annie came by this morning full of sorrow and on the verge of tears. *Max is going to do it,* she said. From the sound of her voice, I pictured something so terrible she couldn't find the words to describe "it."

One of the privileges of getting to be my age is that you can be as outspoken as you pretty well please, so I flat out asked what Max was going to do.

Ruin her life, that's what! *Annie answered.*

The minute I heard that I figured it had something to do with the memories hanging on to poor Max, and I was right.

Annie told me the whole story of how the girl wanted to restore some fellow's memory of their love the way she had restored Oliver's. Over and over again she made the point of how the situation was in no way similar.

Friendship's a tricky thing. If you value it you listen and don't go spouting off advice until it's asked for, so that's what I did. After Annie finished telling her story, she asked what she could do to stop Max.

Not a single thing, *I said and reminded her of how she'd gone back to her boyfriend in Philadelphia. Not once, but twice.*

At the time I worried about her the same way she's worrying about

Max, but if I'd have listed all the reasons for her not giving him a second and third chance she would have retaliated with a list of his virtues. People who think they're in love are blind to anything but what they want to see.

After we'd talked about it for over an hour Annie asked if there was some mix in the apothecary that would keep Max safe, make her immune to anything that lothario whispered in her ear. If it weren't for the fact that she was so dead on serious, I'd have laughed out loud. She's a girl who doesn't believe in her own magic, but she's willing to believe in mine. How funny is that?

Unfortunately, the problem with charms and potions is that you never know exactly how something is going to work. When Annie went back to Philadelphia that last time, I gave her the heart-shaped locket. I figured it was a talisman of love that could protect her heart from making a bad decision. I knew the locket held some powerful memories, but I surely didn't know it would turn on her as it did.

All of my talk did little to comfort Annie, so in the end I told her where to find the tin of anise and I gave her the recipe for Traveler's Tea. I said, Mixed properly this will enable a person to make wise decisions. *She seemed satisfied enough with that thought.*

It's been a very long time since I used that tin of anise, so God only knows if it will even work. The important thing is that Annie believes it will, and she'll in turn convince Max. Sometimes simply having a belief in something is all a person needs.

THE TRIP

That afternoon Annie goes into the apothecary and follows Ophelia's instructions to the letter. Using the small stepladder she climbs high enough to reach above the top of the storage cabinet and stretches her arm until she feels something: a small box pushed so far back it is hidden in the shadows. She pulls it out, and as Ophelia has said it is covered with rose colored silk. A gold tassel is attached to the lid.

Annie blows the years of dust from the box then gingerly carries it down.

When she lifts the lid the box is only half-full. It contains dried leaves; of what plant Ophelia has refused to say. She takes a handful from the box, crushes them in her palm and drops them into the mortar bowl that waits. She then adds the other ingredients: belladonna, verbena, and bog myrtle to sweeten the taste. Using the white porcelain pestle, she grinds the leaves into the consistency of tea.

Six more days. It is now only six days until Max leaves. Annie can only hope the tea she has created will protect Max and prevent her from making a foolish decision. A decision that might lead to heartbreak.

The mix is poured into a small chiffon bag and then put into a box with a silver infuser nested beside it. This will be Annie's going away gift. She will hand it to Max at the airport.

ON THE SECOND WEDNESDAY OF April Annie drives Max to the airport.

"Just drop me at the departures gate," Max says.

"It's three hours until your flight," Annie argues. Her thought is to park the car and stay with Max until it is time for the flight. This is when she plans to give Max the gift.

Max shakes her head. "Don't bother. I'll check in then settle back with my book and read for a while." It's true she has a book to read, but what she doesn't say is that her thoughts are jumping around so furiously she finds it almost impossible to focus on anything.

When she pulls up at the departures terminal Annie pops the trunk open, climbs out of the car, takes the single suitcase from the trunk and sets it on the sidewalk. Max gets out on the passenger side and stands beside the bag.

Annie pulls the small box from her purse and hands it to Max. "This is something I made for you to take on your trip."

Max lifts the lid, sees the infuser and sniffs the pungent mix. "Definitely not dandelion tea," she says.

"No." Annie laughs. "It's much stronger. It's a tea to protect the traveler."

"No love potion, huh?"

Annie shakes her head. "No love potion," she says, but this is somewhat of a lie. According to Ophelia it is a mix that will keep Max safe and prevent her from making bad decisions, which most likely includes letting Julien back into her life.

"Thank you." Max smiles, but there is both sorrow and happiness in her face. "Wish me success," she says and tucks the box into her carry-on tote.

Annie knows success has a different meaning for each of them. For her it means Max will come home and forget this man who offers nothing but heartache. Still she replies, "With all my heart I do." Then she tugs Max into an embrace.

"Take care of yourself," she whispers. "And most of all come back happy."

This is something Max can't possibly guarantee; yet she does. "Swear to God," she says with a lighthearted laugh then crisscrosses her heart.

"Send a text to let me know you got there safely," Annie adds.

"Okay," Max promises. "Now stop worrying."

Annie doesn't tell Max, but the truth is she can't help worrying. She has a bad feeling about this trip. She has a bad feeling about Julien. It will be eleven days before she sees Max again, and in that amount of time almost anything can happen.

As Annie pulls away from the curb she glances into the rearview mirror to take one last look. Max waves goodbye then disappears into the terminal.

WHEN THE PLANE LIFTS OFF the Richmond airport runway, Max feels her heart flutter inside her chest. She is like a child waiting for the circus to arrive in town. Nine hours, she thinks. Nine short hours, and then what? She has a plan. Perhaps it is not much of a plan, but it is the start of one.

Sitting in seat A next to the window, she watches the airport grow smaller and smaller. The houses become dots and then disappear. Highways several lanes wide shrink to the width of a pencil stroke, and before long she can see only fluffy white clouds. There are almost nine hours to go, and yet Max already feels anxious to be there. She slides her foot from her shoe and rocks it back and forth, remembering the feel of cobblestone walkways.

She reaches into her tote and pulls out the street map of Paris. On the front there is a graphic of the Eiffel Tower, but Max opens the map and folds back the panels one by one. Opened fully it is larger than a spread of *The New York Times,* so she refolds it once and then once again until it is the size of a notebook. Facing out is the Fifth Arrondissement, a neighborhood she once called home. She runs her finger along Saint Germain Boulevard then trails off onto the tiny street where the name is barely visible. Although Rue du Bonne is little more than a dash on the map, she can already picture the triangular stone building with its iron balconies.

She is lost in thought when the man sitting next to her asks, "Is this your first trip to Paris?"

Max looks up; until now she hasn't really noticed him.

"No," she replies. "I spent my junior year of college there, but that was over three years ago."

"Ah yes." He smiles. "It is a city that draws you back, is it not?"

"It certainly is," she answers.

He introduces himself as Claude Barrington then takes a business card from his pocket and hands it to her.

He has a velvety voice and an accent, possibly French but with something else mixed in. British perhaps. In an odd way he reminds Max of her father except he is younger, much younger. Probably in his mid to late thirties. Like most of the other travelers she is dressed in jeans but he is wearing a dark suit, the type a banker would wear.

She turns and allows herself to look into his face; his eyes are the same dark brown as Julien's but wider, more set apart and open. Suddenly Max wishes she had a business card to hand him, but she does not. New business cards are like the office; they are both projects she has left simmering on the back burner.

"I'm Max Martinelli," she says and extends her hand.

He takes it in his, squeezes her fingers ever so gently, then releases it. "A pleasure."

His voice, his eyes, the way his hair is casually brushed back with no part, all of it is so familiar, it is as if she knows him.

"Do you live in Paris?" she asks.

He gives a small laugh. "No," he replies, "like you I am a visitor. I am there to see a friend I attended university with."

"I'm going to Paris to see an old friend also." Max does not mention Julien by name, nor does she explain that she is uncertain whether she will even be able to find him.

"What a delightful coincidence," he says. "We are both travelers from another land and another time."

All along Max knew she was from another land, but she'd not considered it another time. When the pictures of Julien come to mind they seem as close as yesterday or the day before, certainly not another time.

"It's only been three years," she says.

"For me it is five," he replies. "Not so very long, but long enough for much to change."

"Like what?"

He laughs. It is a warm mellow sound. "Is there anything that does not change?" he says. This is a rhetorical question, not one he expects answered. "Back then Juan and I were restless young men who spent the nights drinking wine and boasting of how we would one day climb great mountains."

He smiles, and in his eyes she sees the mistiness of remembering.

"Now," he says, "I am tied to a desk, and Juan has a wife and three little ones. Hardly what those carefree young men expected."

"Are you happy?" she asks. The question is out of her mouth before she stops to consider this may be something too personal to share with a stranger. Close as she is to Annie, the answer to that same question is something she has kept to herself.

There is a tiny moment of hesitation; then he nods. "Yes, I believe we both are." He reaches down for his briefcase and lifts out a book.

Max wants to know more about him, but apparently he is ready to move on to another subject. He speaks of the weather in Paris, the crowds at the airport and the hotel where he will be staying.

"The Hotel Baltimore," he says. "Not far from the Arc de Triomphe."

Max knows the hotel. It is on the right bank, an elegant building with flowering iron balconies and plate glass windows surrounding the lobby. The building rounds the corner of Kieber Avenue, a stone's throw from the Champs Elysées.

"Lovely," she says.

"And you?" he asks.

"The Vendome," she replies. "It's near the Sorbonne. On the left bank." As an afterthought she adds, "My friend teaches at the Sorbonne."

"What subject does she teach?"

Max gives a thin laugh. "She's a he," she says, "and he teaches...um...English." Even as she speaks the words she can feel the lie sticking in her throat. *Why?* She wonders. *Why did I have to say that?*

"Nice," he replies politely.

The conversation suddenly goes cold. He opens his book and turns to the page he has marked. He is reading a hard cover copy of *Winter of the World*. The corners of the cover are scuffed and the spine cracked. It is a book that has been read more than once and passed from hand to hand.

"Good story?" she asks.

"Very," he nods. "Have you read anything by Ken Follett?"

"Eye of the Needle," she replies, "but it's been years."

They talk for a short while longer, but now it has segued into the meaningless conversation of strangers. After a few minutes he turns his eyes to the book, and Max retrieves hers from her tote.

In time the cart comes by. Claude orders a scotch then turns to Max. "Can I buy you a drink?"

"Red wine," she replies and thanks him. She hopes he will continue their earlier conversation, but once the drinks are served he goes back to his book.

When the clatter of dinner trays finally subsides, Max closes her eyes.

THOUGHTS OF JULIEN COME EASILY. It is too early for summer, and yet it seems to be summer. He wears a silk tee shirt that clings to his chest like a shadow. She is in a sundress with narrow straps across her bare shoulders. He curls his arm around her and allows his fingertips to rest against the swell of her breast. He brushes a lazy kiss along the side of her neck and laughs.

"Too soon summer will be gone," he says. "The days of love are always too short."

He is the same as she remembers: a shock of dark hair falling carelessly across his brow, a look of intensity stretched tight across his face.

"You promised that you would come," she says.

"Ah, but that was yesterday," he replies. "Now we speak only of today."

They cross the park and turn onto Place St. Michel. Nothing

has changed. A vendor stands on the corner selling fruit from his garden; a little boy pushes past on a scooter.

"What about tomorrow?" she asks.

"Tomorrow is tomorrow," he laughs. "Who can say what is tomorrow. Lovers must live for only the moment that is now."

One question leads to another but there are no answers, only more questions.

"Is it right that I came?" she asks.

He laughs. It is a harsh sound. No longer his voice.

The voice comes again, and she wakes.

The plane has gone from darkness into light. It is now morning. The sound she hears is the crackling of a loud speaker.

"Good morning, madames and messieurs. This is your captain speaking. I am pleased to inform you that we will be landing at Charles de Gaulle Airport in Paris in forty-five minutes. The forecast for today is sunny with a temperature of fifty degrees Fahrenheit or 10 degrees Celsius."

THE FIRST DAY

Once Max has claimed her suitcase, she wheels it through the terminal and follows the signs toward Passport Verification. She has not seen Claude since they left the plane. He was not at the luggage carousel, so he must have come with only a carry-on. There is a moment of disappointment, but she shrugs it off and takes her place in the long line of arrivals. When it is her turn she moves to the window and hands the agent her passport.

He opens it, looks at the picture, then back at her. "Are you here for vacation, mademoiselle?"

It is not truly a vacation; it is a search. She is looking for her past and quite possibly her future, but this is not something she wants to share so she returns his smile and nods. He wishes her a pleasant stay, returns her passport and waves the next person forward.

When Max steps to the curb and hails a taxi she is reminded of four years earlier, the day she'd first arrived in Paris. At the time she'd known almost no French. She'd hauled her suitcase through the terminal, asking directions and searching out signs that led to the RER train.

BACK THEN THERE HAD BEEN time but little money. She received an allowance, enough for food and a room so small she could barely turn around. There were no luxuries. But she hadn't needed luxuries. Simply walking along Saint Germaine Boulevard and through the winding back streets of the Latin Quarter was itself a luxury. To enjoy life in Paris the only things an aspiring architect needed were a sketchpad, a box of charcoals, a laptop and a map of the city.

It was on one of her many excursions that she met Julien.

The sun was warm that day, and she'd walked for miles looking up at the sloping shingled roofs and terraced buildings with ironwork balconies. She first noticed him as she strolled past the Café du Marché on Rue Cler. He was sitting at a small outdoor table. Alone. As she passed by he gave her a smile, a flirtatious look that caused her to blush. Unsure of herself, she returned his smile with a friendly nod and continued walking. He remained in his seat and did nothing until she had moved two stalls down. Then he came running after her flitting a lace hankie in the air.

"Mademoiselle, mademoiselle," he called out.

She somehow knew he was calling her, so she stopped and turned.

He gave her the smile again, the one that could turn a girl's knees to butter.

"I believe you dropped this," he said, offering the hankie.

"You are most kind, monsieur," she replied, "but I am afraid the handkerchief is not mine."

"Are you certain?" he asked. The corner of his mouth curled, and his eyes fixed themselves on hers.

When she turned as if to walk away, he fell into step beside her. Moments later he looped his arm through hers.

They spent the remainder of the day together. He walked alongside her, telling of the history behind one building and another. At the corner of Rue du Champ du Mars he pointed to a shop with well-dressed mannequins standing in the window.

"Before the war the most famous book shop in all of Paris was in that very same spot," he said. "But when the Germans occupied the city they shot the owner, threw the books into the street and burned them."

She gasped. "How awful! But surely you were too young to—"

"For sure," he laughed. "But my père and grandpère were not."

That was the first of many such stories. He had a way of telling about the past as if he were there, part of all that happened, a witness to history. Although it was something Max never could explain, he took the excitement of Paris and added a layer of frosting over it. Everything became deeper, sweeter, something that she, like Julien, would forever hold on to.

WHEN MAX CLIMBS INTO THE taxi, she gives the driver the Rue d'Arris address of the Hotel Vendome. It is a narrow building with burgundy-colored awnings. She has passed by the building countless times but never before stayed there. A single night costs 140 euros. When she'd first come to Paris her room had cost only slightly more for the entire month. That was then; this is now. Then she had time but little money. Now she has a bit more money but only a heartbeat worth of time. Ten days; not even a full two weeks.

As the taxi leaves the airport and eases into the bumper-to-bumper traffic, Max wonders if this meager amount of time is enough to find Julien. Paris has somehow grown bigger, busier. More people crowd the airport, and more cars slow the traffic. There is the constant wonk-wonk of police cars and a rushed feeling that leaps from one car to the next.

She wants to believe this is only because they are near the airport, that when she gets to Rue du Bonne it will be as it always was. She remembers the words of Claude Barrington—*So much has changed*—and worries that her expectations are at best only frail hopes. Is it even realistic to believe that in the short span of ten days two people can fall in love again?

ALMOST A FULL DAY HAS passed since she left home and she has slept only two hours on the plane, yet she is not tired. Once she is in her room at the Hotel Vendome, she throws open the windows and looks down on the street. It is April, a month when the weather is fickle, cold one moment, warm the next. The morning air is cool, and a stiff breeze convinces her to change into something warmer.

After a hot shower she dresses in black slacks, boots and a leather jacket. She winds a red scarf around her neck, a scarf she has worn many times before.

It came from the tiny shop on Rue Bouchard. Although the scarf has remained in the bottom drawer of her dresser for nearly three years, the feel of it around her throat still causes a sting of guilt.

If Annie or Ophelia were to touch the scarf, they would most certainly feel the prickle of the memory it carries. Max already knows it. She remembers the day Julien gave it to her.

IT WAS EARLY DECEMBER, BUT the wind was sharp and the temperature had plummeted to minus 14. Max shivered and snuggled closer to Julien as they walked.

When they passed the expensive Les Femme Bouchard Shop,

the scarf was wrapped around the neck of the mannequin that stood in the window. They stopped to admire it.

"Red." Julien smiled. "A color of passion."

He playfully pulled her into the shop and asked the clerk to take the scarf from the window for Max to try on. She swirled it around her throat, and he beamed.

"Beautiful, so beautiful," he said. "You must have it!"

Max peeked at the price tag and shook her head. The scarf was 48 euros, marked down from 99. That was as much as she spent on food for three days, maybe four.

"I don't think so," she said, then removed the scarf and set it back on the counter.

Julien gave a grimace of disappointment. "Right, red is not for you," he said offhandedly. "Perhaps blue or yellow." He held the scarf alongside her face then gave a disapproving headshake and sent the clerk off to search for something more to his liking.

For nearly an hour they remained in the shop, trying on scarves of every design and color. One by one he wrapped them around her neck, then with an air of disappointment gave another shake of his head. As he removed each scarf he placed it in the growing pile on the counter. First he called for all the solids, then stripes and plaids and in the end there was even one with embroidered forget-me-nots.

When they finally left the counter was piled high with scarves of every color, yet they had purchased nothing.

As they walked along Rue du Bac, Julien leaned down and whispered in her ear.

"Red is the color of a lover's passion." He reached into the inside pocket of his coat, pulled out the red scarf and handed it to her. "And to you I give my passion!" He laughed.

Max gasped. She knew he had not bought the scarf; he had simply taken it. Now he was giving it to her. It was wrong, terribly wrong, and yet delightfully romantic.

"You took this without paying? Are you crazy? You could have been caught and arrested!"

"Ah, but I wasn't," he replied. He yanked the price tag from the scarf then wound it around her neck. When she tried to protest, he covered her mouth with his.

In the days that followed, Max tried to forget the scarf was stolen. Sometimes she even thought about returning it to the store but, right or wrong, Julien had meant it as an expression of his love. He had no money, so he'd gotten her the scarf the only way he knew how.

For weeks on end she economized. She bought day-old bread, went without new charcoals and walked instead of taking the metro. By the middle of January she'd saved up 48 euros and went back to the store.

A different clerk was behind the counter.

"I'm looking for the sales clerk with auburn hair," she said. "She's my height, maybe a snip taller. You know her?"

The clerk shook her head and gave a puzzled shrug. "I only started last week."

"Oh." Max sighed. "You have any idea where she went?"

The clerk again shook her head. "She left before I came."

Max gave another sigh, her disappointment obvious. "She waited on us last time and I was hoping—"

"I can help you," the clerk volunteered.

"It seems there's been a mistake," Max explained; then she said the last time they were in the store they somehow walked out with the red scarf. There was no mention of Julien's name.

"My friend intended to pay for it but forgot." She handed the clerk 48 euros.

"I need the tag," the girl said. "I can't ring up a sale unless I enter what the item is."

"It was a red scarf," Max replied. "Sort of like the blue one in the window."

"That one is 79 euros. It's not the same." The clerk's voice was impatient, testy almost.

"I don't have the tag," Max said. "Can't you just ring up red scarf 48 euros?"

"That's not how we do things! I have to scan the code!"

"You can't ring up 48 euros and say there was no tag?"

"Not unless I'm looking to get fired."

Max stuffed the money in her jacket pocket and left the store.

Two days later she walked across the bridge up the long hill to Sacre Coeur and dropped the 48 euros into the poor box.

Even that did little to assuage her conscience. For months she worried that the girl with auburn hair had been fired because of the stolen scarf.

PUSHING ASIDE THE MEMORY MAX leaves the hotel, walks to the corner and crosses over to Saint Germain Boulevard. She knows the way; she has walked it a thousand times before. She is headed for the tiny street called Rue du Bonne. It is a cluster of only six buildings, an alleyway given a street name. There are several cobblestones set crookedly into the sidewalk that rounds the corner. One stone pokes up and the other is wedged beneath it so the walkway is uneven. A number of times she turned her ankle in this very spot, but what was once a nuisance is now a welcome sign of familiarity. She moves past the first building and, before she reaches number four, senses the change. When she looks up, she gasps. The wooden door is gone, replaced by an entrance made of glass and polished brass.

Alongside this monstrosity there is a keypad. A security device to keep strangers out. A sinking feeling settles in her heart. Max wants to pound on the door and explain that she is not a stranger. She spent almost a year of her life in this building, carrying groceries up the three flights of stairs, preparing meals on the faulty cook stove, washing dishes in water that most days was barely lukewarm.

I am not a stranger, her heart says. *I am not a stranger.*

Max cups her hands to her eyes and peers through the glass. She hopes to see a familiar face, a friend or one-time neighbor. Three years ago she knew almost all of the residents. It's possible that one or two of them have moved away but surely not everyone.

Beside the keypad there is a list of residents. Less names than before and not one she recognizes. Only the names and the keypad code are listed, no apartment numbers. Julien Marceau is not on the list.

Max stands there for several minutes, waiting, but for what she can't say. In time a young man exits the building and turns down the street. Before the door clicks shut her arm shoots out and snags it.

Once inside she discovers there is now an elevator, a tiny thing that at best holds two or three people. It is beside the staircase in a spot where Alfonse, the building manager, once had an apartment. His name is also not on the list of tenants. She passes the elevator by and climbs the stairs. It is a habit hard to break.

On the third floor a wall now covers the spot where a door once led to Apartment D; E is also missing. Three years ago there were five apartments plus a shared bathroom on this floor. Now there are only three. She raps on the door to apartment C where Julien once lived.

A dog barks. A baby cries. "Un moment, s'il vous plaît," a voice calls out.

Moments later a woman opens the door. She is bouncing the baby on her shoulder.

"Oui?" she says.

"I hope I haven't disturbed you," Max replies. Following the woman's lead she speaks French, but hers is clumsy and has the sound of an American. The woman smiles and shuffles the baby from one shoulder to the other.

"No problem," she says. This time she answers in English.

Max explains that she used to live in this apartment and was looking to find some of her old neighbors.

"So you were here before the fire?"

"Fire?"

"Two-and-half, maybe three years ago. It did so much damage they had to refurbish the whole building."

"So that's why some of the apartments are gone."

The woman nods again and asks if she would like to see what they've done.

"Very much," Max replies and follows the woman inside.

She wants to feel the homecoming of being in this place again, but nothing is as it was. The walls are now smooth and the floor a light oak color. The old stove with two small burners and a faulty pilot light is gone. In its place there is a sleek stainless steel kitchen with a full-size refrigerator and dishwasher.

"Oh wow," Max says. "This is beautiful." Although she seems pleased, the truth is she misses the unreliable old stove and the tiny refrigerator that was squeezed in under the counter.

When the baby stops whimpering, the woman extends a hand and introduces herself as Marie. She offers coffee and Max accepts.

Everything has changed but still she is glad to be here, even if it is only for a few minutes. She has yet to ask about Julien or Madame DuBois, the widow who lived at the end of the hall.

As they sit at the small table and sip coffee, Marie explains that the fire was due to a fault in the building's electrical system. It snaked its way up the walls and in the dead of night sent the residents running into the street. By the time the fire department arrived, there was little worth saving.

"Was anyone injured?" Max asks.

"Oui. An elderly gentleman from floor five. I believe he died," Marie says.

Julien is certainly not elderly and his apartment was here on three, but still Max asks, "Do you know his name?"

"Non," Marie answers. "The fire was long before we came here."

WHEN MAX LEAVES THE BUILDING she is heavy of heart.

It is unlikely Julien was the person injured, yet there is still a question. It seems there's never an answer, just a constantly-growing stack of questions.

MAX

I never thought this would be easy, but I didn't think it would be as hard as it is. I guess I expected to see some familiar faces and have the feeling of returning home. Instead I'm a stranger.

Not one of the people I knew is still in the building. I looked at the directory of names and thought, How can that be? How can a whole community of people just vanish? A community, that's what the people who lived there were. Everyone knew everyone, and if you needed something you just knocked on your neighbor's door and borrowed it. We weren't all best friends, but we were a community.

I remember how the Widow DuBois was always hugging people. It didn't matter if you were in a hurry or carrying an armload of groceries, she'd wrap both arms around you and squeeze as hard as she could. She'd hang on for a few seconds then let go and laugh like that was the happiest moment of her day.

Julien used to say she was a nuisance, but the truth is I kind of liked it. She made everybody feel loved. Well, everybody other than Julien; he didn't feel loved, just annoyed.

Today if she ran out and squashed me up against her bosom, I swear I'd hug her right back and I'd kiss that sweet old face. Sometimes you don't realize how good a thing is until you don't have it anymore.

Of course when you're looking back, you only remember the good parts. You forget things like having to wait for the bathroom because somebody was soaking in the tub or wearing two pairs of woolen socks because the floor was icy cold all winter. When I saw Marie's stainless steel kitchen I thought, What a shame, the old cook stove is gone. *How crazy is that? You know sentimentality is getting the best of you when you start feeling blue over a beat-up old stove that refused to work more often than not.*

Marie didn't have any complaints about her kitchen, so I guess the building being redone is a good thing.

But for me it's still sad.

ONE DAY TURNS TO TWO

After she leaves the building Max walks north for several blocks and then turns onto Saint Germain Boulevard. It's a broad street with cafés, bistros and shops on both sides. A street where people come to stroll, shop in markets, linger by the flower stalls or rummage through the long tables of used books. Even though there is a chill in the air, they still sit in the outdoor cafés to sip coffee or linger over a glass of wine.

Max walks slowly and searches the faces that pass by. She hopes to find a familiar one, someone who can say what happened the night of the fire. Someone who knows where Julien is now living.

When she glances down at her watch it is almost seven and yet still daylight. Summer is coming; already the days are growing longer. Back in Wyattsville it is only one o'clock in the afternoon, and yet the weariness of this long day is weighing on her.

She has not eaten since early this morning on the plane, a dry roll with slices of ham and cheese. The smell of food is enticing. She can almost taste the chunks of crusty bread and bubbling onion soup topped with melted Gruyere. At the Café Mabillon, she turns in.

Like the others, she sits at an outdoor table. She is thinking she will have coffee, and yet when the waiter comes she orders a glass of wine.

"Saint Emilion," she says. It is less expensive than the other choices but comes with fond memories.

As Max sips the dark red wine her thoughts slide back to the night of the fire. She can picture people frantically scampering down the narrow staircase. Peter clutching his violin case and Madame DuBois holding tight to the handrail.

She knew all of the residents, but it now seems impossible to separate those who lived on the fifth floor from those who lived on two and four. The third floor she is certain of: Madame DuBois in apartment E, Marianne across the hall in B, Peter a music student from the Netherlands in A, and in D the young waiter who worked in the Café Rouge.

Someone died. Someone—but who? Marie said it was a man from the fifth floor but the fire occurred in 2011, the same year she returned to America. She left Paris in early September, so it had to be after that. Later that month? In the icy cold of winter? Maybe Marie has the year wrong; maybe it was 2012. Maybe this, maybe that. The questions pile one on top of another until they form a staggering mound.

As the chill of evening settles around her, Max sits at the table and ponders her next move. It is not enough to know there was a fire; she needs to know the outcome. It is too late now, but tomorrow she will visit Library Sainte-Genevieve and search for a newspaper account of what happened.

When the weariness of this day pushes against her eyelids, Max returns to the hotel and falls into bed. The window is open, and sounds of the street lull her to sleep.

IT IS NOT YET DAYLIGHT when Max wakes. She feels the crisp air coming from the window and snuggles under the comforter for a few minutes longer. She would like to close her eyes and return to the sweetness of her dream, but it is too late. Her thoughts are already reminding her of what is ahead this day.

First a shower. She twists the faucet handle and waits for the water to grow warm. It has been over three years since she sat in the Sainte Genevieve Library and studied under a yellow lamp at the long wooden table. She is anxious to return. To once again be inspired by the arched windows and ironwork of the upper reading room, to feel the decades of scholars who came before her and the untold numbers who will come after. For any architect the design of the building is something to be admired; for Max it is even more. It is the place that opened her mind to creativity. To again climb the marble staircase will be like returning home.

She dresses in layers: a silk shirt, a wool sweater, a leather jacket that will come off when the afternoon sun grows warm and the red scarf.

When she leaves the hotel she stops for coffee and a croissant at the boulangerie then hurries down Rue Valette and crosses over in front of the Pantheon.

Entering the library, she moves past the seemingly endless rows of stacks on the lower level and heads for the center vestibule and the stairway that leads to the upper reading room.

Once she is settled Max spends the entire morning going through the microfiche files of newspapers for September and October of 2011. Page by page she flips through *Le Petite Parisian*, *Le Figaro*, *L'Express*, and *Le Monde*. There is nothing. Not one word of a fire, an injury or a death in the building. In fact there is no mention of the building at all.

She then expands her search; December of 2011 through the end of 2012.

When this yields nothing she tries Julien's name. Julien

Marceau, she types in, with the range of years 2011-2015. There are two responses. The first is a French resistance fighter who passed away leaving behind two daughters and nine grandchildren. The article tells of his heroic underground effort and ultimate capture by the Nazis. The second find is a doctor who has improved the process of artificial joint replacement. Neither of them are the person she is looking for.

IN THE FIVE HOURS MAX has spent at the library, the sun has all but disappeared. The sky is dark gray with clouds so low they crowd the chimney tops. She pulls the scarf higher around her neck and steps out into the street.

Her next stop will be Magasin Sennelier, the shop where she and Julien bought paper and charcoals. An artist will give up food before they go without the means to draw, so it is likely Julien still goes there. She is warmed by thoughts of Celeste, a woman with a plump grandmotherly bosom and a laugh bigger than that bosom. Celeste was always fond of Julien; she is sure to know where he is.

At the corner of Saint Germain Max hurries down the steps to the metro. It is good to be out of the chilly air and away from the wind whipping her back. She slides her credit card and buys a ten pack of metro tickets.

The Magasin Sennelier Shop is only two stops away on the metro. Three years earlier she would have braced herself and walked the fifteen blocks, but everything is different now; she no longer has the luxury of time. She no longer has Julien walking beside her, tucking her icy cold hand into his pocket.

When the train pulls into the station she climbs on. The car is crowded, but there is music. It comes from a young man with an accordion. Max does not recognize the song, but she does recognize the look of hunger in his eyes. No doubt a music student, as was Peter. The train rattles past Tulleries and screeches to a stop at Concorde. Max drops a two-euro coin in the lad's cup then pushes through the crowd to exit the train.

She hurries up the stairs and along the street. Before she is fully into the shop she has already caught the familiar scents of paper, pastels and charcoals. These odors are far sweeter than perfume; they are reminders of something she loves. At the end of an aisle lined with jars of paint and racks of canvas she spots a woman at the counter—not Celeste, but a young girl with a twist of hair pinned to the top of her head. She is talking with a customer. Max leisurely meanders down the aisle of pastels and waits.

Time does not exist in this shop, so it is easy to recall the feel of a charcoal stick in her hand. Back then she used charcoals and drew on paper with a pebbly grain; now it is mostly pen and ink or computer-generated renderings. Max gives a nostalgic sigh then reaches up and touches her hand to a stick of ochre #4; it is like a smear of mustard on her fingers and she smiles.

"Bonjour."

Startled from her thoughts, Max turns. It is the young clerk.

"May I help you?" she asks.

"I am looking for Madame Celeste," Max says. "Does she still own the shop?"

"Oui, but she is not here today," the girl says. "Tomorrow, she will be here. If you need pastels I can help you."

Max answers the girl with a smile that is soft and easy. "No need. I'm an old friend of Celeste. It's been years since I last saw her, so I wanted to stop by and say hello."

The girl gives an understanding nod. "Oui. Tomorrow then?"

"Yes, tomorrow," Max replies.

MAX LEAVES THE SHOP CHEERED by the thought that tomorrow she will see Celeste. Despite a wind that is too cold for April, she walks back to Rue du Bonne and strolls through the neighborhood.

Once again she searches for a familiar face, but there is none. The bookstall is now a shop of shoes and women's dresses. The wine store is there, but the owners are new. At the flower market Max stops in and finds Suzanne. The old woman remembers her and gives her a hug.

"You are again in Paris?" Suzanne says.

Max shakes her head ruefully. "Only for two weeks."

They talk for a while and Max asks if she has seen or heard from Julien. Suzanne tilts her head back and laughs.

"Julien is not one to visit a shop of flowers," she says.

WHEN DUSK SETTLES IN THE sky, Max remembers that she has not eaten since early this morning. She stops in the small brasserie that three years ago was a charcuterie with featherless ducks and sausages hanging in the window. Outside there are a few patrons sitting at tables. They wear scarves with their collars tugged up around their neck, but they are Parisians and accustomed to the chill.

She goes inside and sits at a small table beside the window. Her stomach is empty, but she is not yet ready for food. She orders a glass of wine and watches the street.

She wants to believe this is the same Paris she left three years earlier. A city crowded with people and yet filled with intimate relationships. Lovers embracing at the metro station, friends gathering for coffee, waiters who sensed what you were going to order before you spoke. These things are the same now as they were three years ago, possibly even a decade ago. Yet so much has changed, in ways that cannot be seen. Only felt.

Max gives a heartfelt sigh and downs the remainder of her wine. Tomorrow is another day, she tells herself. Tomorrow she will visit Celeste and hopefully find Julien.

THE THIRD DAY

On Saturday morning Max arrives at the Magasin Sennelier Shop before it is open. The rolling gate is still padlocked in place. She peers through the metal bars but sees no lights. It is not yet nine, too early for the shops to open. She will go for coffee and return later.

Max turns away and tugs her scarf close around her neck. Many things have changed, but the sharp morning wind is a constant. It pinches her skin now just as it did years earlier. As she hurries off, she glances toward the far end of Quai Voltaire and sees a familiar figure rounding the corner.

"Celeste?" she calls out.

The woman stops and looks up. "Oui?"

With long quick strides she starts toward the woman. "It's me, Max!"

"Max?" The woman fishes in her pocket, pulls out a pair of glasses and slides them onto her nose. "Ah, Maxine!" she laughs. "An old woman's eyes and ears are not so good."

"It's been over three years," Max says with a grin. "I'm delighted that you remembered me at all."

Celeste laughs. It is the same fat round laugh Max remembers.

"And why would I not remember? My eyes and ears are not so good, but my memory is sharp like a young goat."

"It's so good to see you." Max hooks her arm through Celeste's and they walk together.

Celeste fondly tugs Max's arm in closer. "So in New York you are now famous artist?"

Max chuckles. "Hardly. I'm a struggling architect in Virginia."

"Ah yes, architect," Celeste murmurs. "A designer of buildings."

"So far it's been mostly showrooms and home additions," Max replies, "but I'm still hopeful."

Celeste gives Max's arm a squeeze. "In time," she says. "All things come in their right time; for now you are here and it is enough."

"Actually I'm here because I'm looking for someone."

"The blonde girl, Babeth?"

"No, Julien Marceau. I thought maybe you'd know where—"

Before Max can finish the question, Celeste comes to an abrupt stop and turns to her.

"Why you bother with him?" she asks. Her face appears less round; her chin is squared, and her brows lowered in a way that shades her eyes.

The question rattles Max. Maybe it's not the question but the tone in which it is asked.

"He's a friend," she says hesitantly. "But I haven't seen him for over three years—"

"Better you leave the past to the past," Celeste snaps. She again starts toward the shop, her steps now quicker and more purposeful.

"You liked Julien, why would you say—"

"I say only the past is the past."

"Did he say something or do something?"

Celeste narrows her eyes, and when she speaks Max sees little of the woman she knew.

"It is true I am an old woman," she says, "but not so old that I

65

cannot see when a man slides brushes and charcoals into his pocket."

Max cringes when she hears this. Her thoughts jump to the red scarf and she fears there is some truth to Celeste's words, but still she defends Julien.

"He can be forgetful," she says. "I'm sure he meant to pay, but got distracted—"

Celeste's expression is one of disdain. "I doubt that."

"When I find Julien, I'll tell him about this. I'm sure he will—"

"You won't find him unless he wants you to find him."

Max's voice grows thin, like a sound carried off by the wind. The certainty in Celeste's words is unnerving. "Why? Why will I not find him?"

"He is a shadow that comes in sunlight and disappears in darkness."

"Julien?"

Celeste gives a thunderous sigh and nods.

Max is relentless. She has come all this way and is not ready to give up. "How can you say that? When was the last time you saw him?"

The softness is now gone from Celeste's face. "Two years," she says sourly, "or more."

"And where did he live then?"

"In the building burned out a year earlier." Celeste gives a bitter laugh. "Or at least that was the address he wrote on his charge account."

Max gasps. "We lived there together." Her hand flies to her heart. "Dear God," she murmurs. "After the fire he had nowhere else to go…"

Celeste gives her head a doubtful shake then bends down and slides a key into the padlock at the bottom of the drawn gate. She lifts it enough to scoot under then pulls it back down again, leaving Max outside.

"Wait—"

Celeste turns back one last time.

"You're a good girl, Maxine," she says. "Go home and design buildings; don't get mixed up in this." With those words she disappears inside the store.

"Get mixed up in what?" Max asks, but it is a pitiful cry that goes unheard.

MAX STEPS TO THE SIDE and waits. When the store opens she will ask Celeste what the words meant. Nine o'clock comes and goes, but the gate remains closed. It is almost ten when the young girl comes, unlocks the gate and goes in. A few minutes later the lights go on and the gate is rolled up. Max goes inside. The girl is again behind the counter.

Max walks over and says, "I'd like to speak to Madame Celeste."

"Sorry," the girl replies. "She's not here."

"But..."

It is too late; the girl turns her back and walks away.

WHEN MAX LEAVES THE SHOP her heart is thundering in her chest. Try as she may she cannot shut out the sound of Celeste's words. The best she can do is not believe them. She walks along the Quai to Rue du Bac then turns right toward Boulevard Saint Germain. It feels as though her feet are made of lead; they are weights that cause her knees to tremble when she steps down from a curb. Still, she continues to move forward because right now she needs to be in the area she knows. She needs to be close to Rue du Bonne.

It is unthinkable that all the residents of the building have moved away. People don't leave a neighborhood they've known forever. *They're still there,* she tells herself. In a different building, perhaps a block to the east or five doors to the west, but somewhere close by. They are still a community; only she is missing. It is simply a matter of time until she spots a familiar face: Peter, Marianne or the Widow DuBois. The chubby old woman from the second floor. The pregnant girl from 5B, who by now would have a toddler.

As she walks Max brings to mind the faces of the people from the other floors: Alfonse, the building manager, Claire and her younger sister. She counts them as she remembers—twenty-five, and then thirty. Thirty people, but she only needs to find one of them. Where she finds one, she will find them all.

THE HOURS DRAG BY AS Max zigzags in and out of the twisting streets surrounding Rue du Bonne. She looks at every face, tries to imagine if this man had a beard, if that woman were blonde, if a toddler resembles the brunette from 5B. It is like putting a jigsaw puzzle together when you know nothing of what the picture should look like.

It is after five when she feels the rumbling of her empty stomach and stops in at the Café Rouge. All day she has rattled her brain but cannot remember the name of the young waiter from 3D. She can picture his face: narrow with close-set eyes and a sharp nose. A pleasant enough face but one that can only be described as ordinary.

The day has grown warmer, so Max sits at an outdoor table. The weather is one of the few things that hasn't changed. Although it is springtime, Paris is still cold in the morning with a sharp wind that whistles along the narrow streets. By early afternoon spots of sun dapple the sidewalks, and the outdoor cafés come alive.

When the waiter arrives she orders coffee, then changes it to wine.

"There used to be a young man who worked here," she says, "tall, thin face, brown hair. Sound familiar?"

The waiter shrugs. "Georges maybe, or Henri?"

Neither name sounds familiar. Max shakes her head. "It was about three years ago."

"Before me," the waiter says. "Henri is in the back. Wait, I will ask."

Max nods and gives him a smile. "Merci."

Moments later Henri comes out. He recognizes Max, bends down, kisses her on both cheeks then lowers himself, into the chair beside her. "So I understand you are looking for someone."

"About three years ago, a young man who lived in the same building as me—number four, Rue du Bonne—worked here. I can't recall his name but—"

"Gilles Lemonde," Henri says. There is a note of sadness attached to his words.

Max smiles. "Yes, that's it. Gilles. Is he still here or do you know where—" Noticing the look on Henri's face she stops. "What? Is something wrong?"

"Gilles is dead. Killed. December before last in a motorbike accident. I am sorry to be the one to—"

Max lets go of a heartfelt sigh. "Oh, how terribly sad. We were only casual friends, but I am sorry to hear of his death. He was a nice young man."

They spend a few moments longer speaking of Gilles, but death is an unpleasant subject so as soon as he can Henri squirms away.

"I am needed in the kitchen," he says, but the truth is he simply does not want to be here talking of this.

Although Max seldom saw Gilles more than once a week and even then it was simply a passing hello, she still mourns his loss. Whether it is because a young life was squashed out far too soon or because his absence is another brick wall in her search, she cannot say. It is impossible to sort through the reasons; she knows only that a weight of sadness has settled on her shoulders.

She orders a plate of asparagus crepes but barely picks at it. She remembers the small Honda Julien rode. It was much smaller than Gilles's bike. And, she thinks, far more dangerous.

MAX

B efore I left Wyattsville Annie told me that after her mother died she kept going back to the places they'd gone together. The same restaurant, the same beauty parlor. She even went crosstown to the same library. She claims doing that was a big mistake.

It was never the same, according to Annie, and going back spoiled her good memories. She said when you're happy and having a good time you can't see the imperfections of a place, but if you go back and look at it with a critical eye trying to figure out what it was that you enjoyed so much you'll discover it's nothing like you remembered. I'm beginning to wonder if maybe she isn't right.

I had such good memories of that year — of Julien and the people in the building. Now it seems like those memories are being pushed aside. The building is different, the people are gone and poor Gilles is dead. We weren't close friends, but he made me feel good with his big smile and a happy "Bonjour!" I wish I could go on thinking of him that way, but now that's impossible.

And to hear Celeste speak of Julien as she did was like a knife in my heart. After the incident with the scarf I suspected he stole other things, but I was happy believing it was just that one time and only because he loved me. If he did take the brushes, it was only because he needed them

71

desperately and had no money. He's an artist, and for an artist being without brushes is like losing an arm. Besides, there's always the possibility Celeste was wrong. Even she admits she's getting old and has poor eyesight.

Julien may have his faults, but he's a loving man. He cares about people and would never do anything to intentionally hurt someone.

Once when we were walking through the Tulleries he found a small bird with a broken wing on the side of the pathway. It was an icy cold January day and the bird would have frozen to death if it remained there, but Julien picked it up, carried it back to the apartment and nursed it back to health. He used two toothpicks and made this teeny, tiny splint. If you could have seen the tender way he handled that bird, you'd know he's not a bad person. A bad person would never have the patience to care for a living thing the way he cared for that bird. Okay, I'll admit Julien may have his faults, but it's only because he's had a hard life.

I hope to God I find him. If I do, I'm going to ask him to come back to America with me. I'll say whenever he needs brushes I'll buy them. An artist shouldn't have to steal the brushes he needs to paint.

THE SKATEBOARD INCIDENT

Sunday morning dawns with a thick curtain of rain covering the city. Before she is fully awake Max sees the gray sky. She climbs from the bed and pushes open the window. A gust of cold damp air pushes back. She slams the window shut and twists the lock. This is the kind of day meant for crawling back into bed and snuggling under the comforter.

Three years ago that's exactly what she would have done, but not today. With only seven days left she wants to make every minute count. She had hoped to have already located Julien and by now be spending these precious hours with him; instead she is still searching.

She trudges to the bathroom, turns the shower on and waits for it to grow warm. When a cloud of steam fills the room she steps in and lets the water cascade across her shoulders.

Today Max is uncertain where this search will lead her. She has no starting point, and the rain will surely keep people inside. As she towels herself, she tries to remember what Julien did on days such as this. More often than not he climbed back into bed and tugged her down beside him; but there were other times, times when he went out to sell his sketches.

She pictures him in the dark brown parka, a hood pulled over his head and a portfolio of sketches tucked beneath his arm. He laughs and says, *Even an artist must eat.* The picture is clear in her mind, but where he goes now is still a mystery.

On sunny days he would go to the Quai Branly beside the Seine and watch for tourists. Often he unfolded a pad to sketch as he waited. It was a way to entice the passersby to stop. Parisians ignored him; a dime a dozen, they'd say and keep walking. But the tourists stopped. And they often bought.

The price was whatever Julien thought the person had in his or her pocket. For some it was ten euros; for others the same sketch would cost one hundred euros. He had a way of knowing a person's worth. It was as if he could see into their wallet.

Max brushes a bit of gloss on her mouth and decides.

Across from the Quai de la Tournelle there is a long stretch of shops and alcoves. More than once Julien ducked into one of those places escaping the cold or wet weather. He could easily enough charm a shopkeeper into allowing him to sketch their likeness or a clever replica of their front window. Then when a crowd gathered to watch, he sold a few drawings.

Max again dresses in layers. She doubts any of them will be removed on a day such as this, and the layers are warmer. She pulls on jeans, a long-sleeved tee, a wool sweater and a blazer, then covers it all with a hooded poncho. The poncho is bulky and unattractive but will keep her dry. She tosses the folding umbrella in her bag. If the wind dies down she may be able to use it, but this also is doubtful.

Instead of taking the metro, she walks. If she hugs the buildings the wind is less, and there is always the chance she will see a familiar face.

Because of the weather, only a handful of people are on the street and the few she passes rush by hidden beneath hoods or wearing hats pulled low over their face. No one looks up, and peering from beneath her hood Max herself can barely see the faces of those she passes.

This morning La Petit Pontoise has taken in the tables that usually line the sidewalk. The few customers who have braved the elements sit inside. Max joins them, ordering coffee and a croissant. She drops a single sugar cube into the coffee and stirs. The coffee is black and stronger than what she is used to, but she downs it quickly then orders a second. While she is inside she pushes back the hood of her poncho. It is good protection from the rain, but with it pulled over her head it is like seeing the world through a peephole.

As Max leaves the bistro she hears the bells of Notre Dame. It is ten o'clock. She turns toward the river and continues on her way. Her stride is purposeful at first then she slows her step. Every waking moment has been spent in search of Julien, but the bells remind her of Sunday mornings when she and her mother would attend church together. Afterward they would stop at the coffee shop and talk.

She can still remember the sound of her mother's laughter. At the time she was thirteen years old. Unlucky thirteen; the same year her father ran off and left her mother to die of a broken heart.

Instead of turning on Tournelle, she crosses the bridge then turns left toward the front entrance of the cathedral. The Mass is half over by the time she arrives, but today the crowd is thin and there is plenty of room. She slides into a back pew and listens. The Mass is said in French but not truly understandable. It contains too many words that are unfamiliar.

Max listens and for a short time feels at peace. She is not thinking of finding Julien; she is remembering her mother. Remembering the good days, not what came after.

By the time she leaves the cathedral the rain has slowed to a drizzle but it is still windy, too windy for the umbrella. She hooks it onto her wrist, then pulls the hood over her head and makes the return trek across the bridge.

On Quai la de Tournelle there are small clusters of people, tourists mostly. Those who pass her headed east are most likely on their way to see Notre Dame, and those who follow the path she walks are on their way to visit Invalides or the Museum d'Orsay. Three blocks after she has turned onto Tournelle, she catches sight of the figure coming toward her.

A boy on a skateboard. He speeds up. She moves a step to the right trying to get out of his pathway. He then zigs to the left. A second later he slams into her, knocking her to the ground as he throws a chocolate milkshake in her face.

This is not an accident. It is intentional. The liquid splatters in her eyes, and she is momentarily blinded.

Before she can wipe the goo from her face and gather her senses, the boy is gone. Max's hand flies to her face and she feels the sticky mess on her skin. Already she can sense the taste of chocolate on her lips. "Dear God," she moans.

Suddenly she feels it—from behind a man reaches beneath her arms and lifts her to her feet. He shoves a hankie into her hands.

"Use this to wipe that stuff off," he says.

His voice is soft, thick with compassion and familiar enough to cause her heart to flutter.

Without looking, Max takes the hankie and starts dabbing at the thick goo around her eyes.

He speaks again. "A lad doing such a thing is disgraceful..."

Now more than ever she is certain. After two quick swipes across her eyes, she is able to force them open. She lifts her head and sees it is as she thought.

She gasps. "Julien!"

He has the look of a man who has touched his hand to lit coals. He steps back, wide-eyed and fearful looking.

"It's me, Maxine!"

"Maxine?" he says. "How could I not have recognized you?" He makes the words sound as if he is glad to see her, but his expression is one of agony. He hesitantly moves forward and places his hands on her shoulders. He holds her at arm's length and makes no move to draw her to him.

"Mon dieu, Maxine, is this not fate?" he stammers.

A young woman is standing alongside of him. She is a tiny thing with big eyes, stringy black hair and the fragile look of a waif. Max has no idea what the girl's relationship is with Julien. Is she a friend? A sweetheart? A wife perhaps? Although she is standing back a bit, Max glances at her hand. No ring. Probably not a wife. She is too young anyway. She is only fifteen or sixteen. Certainly no more than seventeen.

A thousand times Max has envisioned their meeting, and it was never like this. The words she'd planned are now useless, and she stumbles around searching for the right thing to say.

"I was in Paris," she finally says, "and hoping I'd run into you. I thought maybe—"

He cuts in with another repeat of her name. "Maxine..." The sound of it is foreign and lumbers haphazardly across his tongue. "I wouldn't in a million years expect..." He makes no mention of their past. It is as if she is little more than an old friend, a classmate or perhaps a neighbor.

She tries to smile, but it is impossible to smile when your face is crusted with chocolate milk and your heart is breaking. This may be the only chance she has, so she takes it.

"We have so much to talk about," she says. "Do you think that maybe we could—"

In a pretense of brushing the milkshake from her poncho, he leans in close. "This evening at the café," he whispers. There is no need to say which one. It is understood that it will be the café in Rue Cler, the one where they met.

The young woman moves closer. She bends to pick up the

umbrella and bag Max has dropped then takes a wad of tissues from her pocket and wipes the bag. With the bag still looped over her arm, she pops open the umbrella and shakes the drippings from it.

Moments later she tells Julien, "Hurry up, we've got to get going." Her voice is sharp and riddled with the sound of agitation.

Using Julien's handkerchief, Max takes one last swipe at the front of her poncho then hands the soiled hankie back to him.

He shakes his head and says, "Keep it."

She sees the tears in his eyes. "Julien, it's not too—"

The waif gives an impatient huff, then turns on her heel and starts down the street.

Julien hesitates a moment. He looks into Max's eyes and once again says, "I'm sorry; so very sorry." His voice is thick and choked with emotion. Before she can answer, he turns and follows the waif.

With the handkerchief still in her hand, Max tearfully gives the poncho a few more swipes. When she looks up they have both disappeared.

MAX

I felt like a fool standing in the middle of the street bawling my eyes out, but I couldn't do a thing about it. It was as if the heartache and tears I've held back all these years suddenly spilled over. Once they began, there was no stopping them.

I was broken enough to cry, and when that happens you have to keep right on crying until the brokenness is out of you.

It was more than just Julien. It was my entire life I was crying over. All the stupid things I'd pushed to the back of my mind for God knows how long. I missed Mama, was considered a failure because I didn't have an office, had wasted three years of my life loving a man who didn't even recognize me and was standing there covered in a sticky gooey mess.

It seemed as though some giant hand reached down from the sky, smacked me in the head and said, "Well, Max, now you've done it. You've royally screwed up your life."

The sorry thing is I'm not even sure whether that's true. A lot depends on what Julien has to say tonight. I can't imagine what happened after I left Paris, but I do know that today when he looked at me he remembered how it was with us. If he remembers, then he's got to feel as I do. If not, we can start over. Let it be as it was in the beginning.

On the plane I pictured the moment when Julien and I would meet again. I could see a slow smile sliding across his face and imagine the way he'd walk toward me and take me into his arms as he used to do. I knew after three years there was a possibility he'd met someone else, but I never expected she'd be with him when we saw each other again.

The thing is, he wasn't looking at her. He was looking at me, and he had tears in his eyes. My bet is that she's just a friend or maybe a casual date.

I doubt it's possible he can love her as he did me.

THE LONG WAIT

When the tears subside, Max leaves Quai la de Tournelle and walks back to the hotel. She stops at the front desk long enough to pick up her room key then hurries upstairs.

A quick glance in the mirror shows her poncho is in worse shape than she thought. She pulls it over her head, rolls it into a ball and stuffs it into the wastebasket. There are additional splatters on the blazer and jeans, but these are small enough to sponge off. Once that is done she peels off the remainder of her clothes and steps into the shower. She stands directly beneath the showerhead and lifts her face.

The dried milk is caked in the corners of her eyes, beneath her fingernails, at the edge of her ear and in her hair. Using a washcloth, she scrubs her face over and over again until it is bright pink and tender to touch. She then shampoos her hair three times. Long after the last trace of the milkshake is gone she still feels the slime of it and lathers her body for yet another time. When she finally steps from the shower Max is spent, both emotionally and physically.

Julien said the café this evening. That means seven, six-thirty at the earliest. Three hours to wait, and she is so very tired. Max pulls a bathrobe around her and climbs beneath the comforter. In almost no time she is sound asleep.

THIS TIME THE DREAM IS about her mama. It starts with the ominous sound of a warning. *Be careful what you wish for*, Eugenia Martinelli says. *I wished for your daddy, and he's what I got!* The voice is familiar and yet it is different, sorrowful and heavier than Max remembers.

Once again she and her mama are sitting in the red plastic booth at Bean's Coffee House. The church bells are ringing; they should be crossing Main Street by now. In a few minutes the services will start, and they are still nine blocks away.

Three times Max says they've got to get going, but her mama doesn't move. She sits there dabbing her red-rimmed eyes with a hankie and picking at a loose button on the front of her blouse.

"This isn't an ordinary Sunday," she tells Max. "When we get back to the house your daddy won't be there. He's leaving and never coming home again."

"That's silly, Mama," the thirteen year-old Max replies. "Even when Daddy goes away for work, he always comes home."

"Work?" Eugenia gives a sour laugh. "Baby, you're a fool to believe what he says. He's not working. He's playing house with his other family." Tears fill Eugenia's eyes.

"No, he's not," Max says. Her small hand reaches across the table and holds on to her mama's. "Daddy doesn't really have no other family. He was just saying that 'cause he was mad."

Eugenia dabs her eyes again. It's too late. A tear falls and splashes against the brown Formica tabletop.

"It's unfair, Maxine," she replies. "I know it's unfair. Unfair to you and unfair to me. But your daddy has another wife and another baby. He wants to be with them more than he wants to be with us."

"You're wrong, Mama," Max argues. "Daddy loves me, and he loves you too."

Eugenia shakes her head, her face a rumpled mask of tragedy. "Believe what you want, but the truth is a man like your daddy doesn't love anybody but himself."

"That's not true!" Max shouts. "Daddy loves me! He said he loves me!"

"Don't believe everything you hear," Eugenia says. "If you start listening to the lies of a man like your daddy, one day you'll end up with one who's just the same."

"No!" Max screams. "No, no!"

WHEN SHE PULLS HERSELF FROM the dream Max is trembling and soaked with perspiration. For several minutes she lies there trying to convince herself it was only a dream. It somehow seems too real, too close. She wants to move on, away from the dream, but the words keep running through her mind.

You'll end up with one who's the same.

She glances over and checks the time. Five o'clock. Although pieces of the dream are still clinging to her, she climbs from the bed and takes another shower.

For now the rain has stopped, but the wind is still going strong. She dresses in jeans, a sweater and her leather jacket, then drops the umbrella in her bag and heads out the door.

Tonight she will take the metro. It is almost six o'clock, and she has had enough of walking for this day. At the corner station she descends the stairs and passes through the turnstile. It is

Sunday evening, and only a few people are waiting for the train: an elderly couple, a group of young women and, at the far end of the platform, a boy carrying a skateboard. When Max looks up the electronic timer says it will be two minutes and thirty-seven seconds until the next train arrives.

The skateboard boy moves toward the center of the platform, closer to where the elderly couple stands. Max watches. Already she feels the queasiness spreading from her stomach to her chest. This boy looks taller than the one this morning, but she can't be sure. He is wearing the same type of dark hooded jacket. She tries to picture the face of the boy coming toward her, but it is impossible. His image is nothing more than a speeding blur.

One minute and seventeen seconds until the train arrives.

Max feels the thump-thump-thump of her heart, but her eyes never leave the skateboard boy. If he lowers his board to the ground or moves closer to the couple, she will scream a warning.

The electronic sign flashes zero, and the train roars into the station. Still she watches. The doors whoosh open. The elderly couple and the chatty group of young women climb aboard; the skateboard boy remains on the platform. A split second before the doors close Max steps onto the train. She is in the same car as the elderly couple. As the train pulls out of the station Max catches a closer glimpse of the boy. Now she is certain; he is not the same person.

A different boy, and yet the pounding of her heart continues. *Be afraid*, it warns. *Be afraid of everything and everyone!*

There are empty seats on the train, but Max stands and holds to the metal pole. It is like an anchor holding her in place. She needs to hold on to something, to steady the trembling of her hands.

She reminds herself that the incident of this morning is over and done with; there is nothing left to fear. It was a bad experience, but now it is time to let go and appreciate the good that came from it: finding Julien. Wanting to ease the pressure in her chest, she takes several deep breaths and tries to move her thoughts forward.

It too late; the fear has already settled in.

THREE STOPS LATER SHE EXITS the train at Ecole Militaire. The Café du Marche is two streets down. She crosses over in front of the post office and turns onto Rue Cler. Although it is no longer raining, the air feels raw and damp so she hurries along. Already it is six-thirty.

The tables at the café are still outside, but they are empty. The customers are inside where it is warm and much cozier. For a moment Max considers this, but she worries Julien will pass by and not think to look inside. Too risky. She sits at an outdoor table under the awning, the same one he was sitting at the day they met.

The waiter comes and she orders coffee. It will be something to warm her. She will only be outside for a short while; once Julien arrives they can move inside, perhaps to one of the intimate back tables nestled in the corner. The one behind the pole, she decides. They have much to talk about, and it is quieter at that partially hidden table.

When the coffee comes she lifts the cup and holds it with both hands. The warmth of it feels good but lasts only a few minutes. By the time she finishes it the coffee is ice cold.

Max checks her watch. Seven-ten. Julien will be here any moment. The coffee did little to warm her, so she now orders red wine.

"I am expecting a friend," she tells the waiter, "so bring a bottle of Saint Emilion and two glasses."

"Oui," he answers and scurries off.

Max is pleased with the thought of once again sharing a bottle

85

of wine with Julien. It is what they often did. She closes her eyes and imagines the picture. With long strides and a quick step he will cross the courtyard, late as always. He will smile, rattle off a quick apology, then bend and let his lips land lightly on hers. Afterward he will slide into the seat opposite her, and they will talk.

Soon it is seven-thirty and then eight. The evening air grows cold, and Max pulls the red scarf closer around her neck. Every few moments she stretches her neck and searches the walkway. She is uncertain from which direction he will be coming, so she looks one way and then the other. When the first glass of wine is finished, she pours a second.

Three times the waiter returns and asks if she would like to move inside where it is warmer. "I will watch for your friend," he offers.

Although Max shivers from the cold, she answers no.

"It's quite comfortable here," she lies.

Shortly after nine, the waiter, a man with silver hair and a sizeable paunch, comes with a bowl of beef soup and a basket of bread. Max has ordered nothing but still he sets it on the table and says, "You must eat."

Max protests, saying she will wait for her friend and they will eat together.

The waiter shakes his head and waves off such a suggestion. He repeats, "You must eat," and adds that on such a chilly evening it is not healthy for a person to be without food.

The soup smells good and since she has not eaten since this morning's croissant, Max is hungry. She lifts a spoonful to her mouth and smiles. "Thank you."

He gives a satisfied nod then disappears back inside.

After a few spoonfuls, Max can eat no more. The taste is good, but the pieces of beef are stuck in her chest and refuse to go down. Her stomach is too knotted to accept food. She is beginning to worry that perhaps Julien had a different café in mind. One by one she tries to recall the cafés where they sat across from one another and lingered for hours over a single glass of wine. There are a dozen, perhaps more, each one special in a different way but none with the sentimental significance of the Café du Marche. Since he simply called it the café, it would seem he meant this place.

She checks her watch and continues to wait. It is soon nine-thirty and then ten. Most of the customers from inside have already gone; only one of the tables is still occupied. The waiter comes, frowns at the remaining soup in the bowl then carries it off. When the couple at the last table leaves, the waiter starts to clear away the menus and tablecloths. It is almost eleven, and the café is about to close.

He isn't coming. Something's happened again. The waif perhaps, Max thinks. *I should have told him where I'm staying.*

She wants to trust that since he knows she is in Paris, he will try to find her. If something prevented him from coming tonight, he will surely be here tomorrow.

This is what Max tells herself, but in the back of her mind her mama's voice is screaming, *Fool! Believe in a man such as him, and you'll end up like me.*

Max waves to the waiter and signals for the check. When he comes and hands her the bill it is twenty-eight euros. He has charged her for only the coffee and wine. She thanks him then fumbles through her bag looking for her wallet.

Pushing aside a clutter of tissues, hair clips, notepads, pens and other things, she burrows down to the bottom of the tote. Her wallet is not there. She empties the bag onto the table, and a jumble of things fall loose. The wallet is not among them. Neither is her iPhone. Frantically searching through the pockets of first her jacket and then her jeans, she exclaims, "My wallet is gone!"

"Is it possible you forgot it at the hotel?" the waiter suggests.

Again Max rummages through the pile of clutter on the table. "No, it's not. I had it and my phone with me this morning—"

"Do you remember where you were?" he suggests. "Maybe the wallet fell out of your bag. You could go back and look for it."

Max looks up, wide-eyed. "My phone is gone too!"

He makes a tsk-tsking sound. "These days there are many pickpockets here in Paris," he says sadly. "It is possible..."

"No," she argues, "there was no chance..." She stops, remembering the boy on the skateboard.

The waiter says nothing; he waits and listens. He remembers several years back when his wife's purse was stolen from beneath her nose.

"There was a boy on a skateboard," Max says. "He knocked me down and threw a milkshake in my face, but he was gone in an instant. He didn't have time to—"

The waiter grimaces and gives a nod. "A diversion. The boy was only a ruse. While you were distracted by him, a nearby accomplice reached into your bag and took your things."

"Impossible," she says, "the boy was alone."

He shakes his head in disagreement. "Someone was there," he says. "That's how these pickpockets operate." He tells the story of his wife's purse being stolen.

"She had it right beside her as she was picking out tomatoes at the market when this woman started shouting about the price of one thing or another. She turned to see what all the fuss was about, and when she turned back her bag was gone."

"You're kidding!"

"Not kidding," he says. "The street thieves are quick like lightning!"

Max begins searching her pockets for loose coins. She finds two five euros, a single two-euro and several dimes.

"I don't have twenty-eight euros," she says sorrowfully. "I can give you twelve and then send..."

"Keep it," he replies. "Tonight is no charge." He lifts the check from table, tears it in half and slides both pieces into his pocket.

Max stands, wraps her arms around him and kisses his cheek.

"Thank you," she says. "Thank you so very much."

WHEN MAX LEAVES THE CAFÉ the dampness of the day still hangs in the air, but it is accompanied by the bitter cold of night. Even though it is late, she walks back to the hotel. The streets have grown dark and quiet; the only sound she hears is the clicking of her heels against the cobblestones. A single question settles in her head. *What now?*

If only I could text Annie, she thinks. *She could send money or at least help me figure out what to do.* It is then that she remembers the tea Annie gave her as a parting gift. The words are still in her mind.

It is a brew that protects the traveler.

If ever Max needed protection, it is now.

Tomorrow morning there will be no coffee; there's no money for it anyway. Tomorrow morning she will ask for a pot of hot water, fill the silver infuser with the tea and allow it to steep for a full five minutes. Then she will drink it down to the last drop.

Afterward she will go back to the Petit Pontoise; possibly the wallet and phone fell from her purse when she stopped for coffee. From there she'll go to Notre Dame and check. Afterward she will follow her footsteps along the Quai de la Tournelle to where the accident happened. It was raining, she wasn't paying attention; it's conceivable that her wallet and phone just fell from the bag. Maybe they are still lying there somewhere along the route, pushed to the side of a wall or hidden beneath a trashcan.

It simply makes no sense to think they were stolen because no one else was anywhere close to her. Only Julien and his waif-like friend.

Fool! her mama's voice repeats.

BACK IN BURNSVILLE

Max has been gone for less than a week, yet Annie misses her terribly. Over the past several months they have gotten into the habit of speaking once a day or at least every other day. Often it is about nothing in particular—some new potpourri Annie has discovered or the job Max is working on—but the warmth of friendship is threaded through every conversation.

On Sunday evening she mentions this to Oliver.

"I'm concerned about Max," she says. "I haven't heard from her for three days."

He is hunched over the study desk poring through the transcripts of the custody battle that will start tomorrow morning. He absently replies, "Didn't she text you and say she got there safely?"

"Yes, but I haven't heard from her since."

Oliver looks up and says, "That was just a few days ago."

"I know. But I've got this feeling..."

"It's nothing," he says and returns to his paperwork. "She's probably just busy having fun."

"Unh-uh." Annie shakes her head dubiously. "If everything was good, she'd have written to tell me about it."

Without looking up Oliver says, "Can we talk about it later? This trial starts tomorrow, and I've got to finish going through these reports."

"Okay. Sure." Annie turns away and leaves him to his work. The conversation is over, but there are still a bunch of worrisome thoughts picking at her brain.

AFTER ALL THAT HAS HAPPENED, Annie has learned to trust her instincts. And whether or not there is justification for it, she is starting to believe something has gone wrong.

She and Max have been friends for one short year, but in that year they have grown close as Siamese twins. Although it is as unexplainable as a potpourri that reflects a person's thoughts, their tie to one another has become both physical and emotional. They somehow sense what one another will say before the words are spoken, and thoughts travel between them like telepathic waves.

Although Annie seldom works in the apothecary on Sunday, this particular evening she is inclined to do so. Her head is filled with questions, and none of them have answers. The busyness of blending teas or sorting through tins of herbs is something that brings peace of mind. There is magic in every room of Memory House, but in the apothecary it is more powerful. There Annie finds clarity of vision, and she believes that being there will enable her to see things she might not otherwise see.

Ophelia laughs at such a thought and claims this belief is something Annie hangs on to like a rabbit's foot or a four-leaf clover.

"The magic isn't in the apothecary," she says. "It's in you and what you bring to the apothecary."

Although she has heard this a dozen or more times, Annie is still reluctant to believe it. Her contention is that Ophelia left behind whatever magic there is when she moved out of Memory House. It is like the hall table or the bedroom lamp, left behind for the next occupant to take and use.

Annie's cell phone is in her pocket. She keeps it with her hoping it will beep a text message. Tomorrow will be four days since she last heard from Max. *Too long*, she thinks.

Lifting a tin of dried strawberry leaves from the shelf, she adds a scoop to the mixing bowl and then reaches for the basket of broom flowers. Countless times Herbert Blander has been warned to cut back on steaks and red wine, but he refuses to give them up. Instead he looks to the apothecary for a soothing tea. Annie adds a spoonful of dried cherry bits to sweeten the mix, then pours it into a box marked with Herbert's name.

As she sets this aside she checks her watch: 10PM. It is 4AM in Paris; she knows there will be no message from Max tonight. She pulls the phone from her pocket and settles in the chair alongside the skirted table. She turns the phone on and waits until the message icon pops up, then scrolls back through the list. There is one from Giselle with a picture of the twins, another from a college, an advertisement from Dyson's Drugstore and lastly the message Max sent Thursday morning. She has already read this message, but there is a certain comfort in rereading it. She clicks on Max's name and waits until the text appears on the screen.

> Arrived OK. Trip was good. Met a nice guy on the plane, Claude Barrington. He's staying at the Baltimore Hotel. Fancy place. Must have a few bucks. I'll let you know when I find Julien. Luv, M

She reads the message several times but can find no clue or word of foreboding written between the lines. The logical part of her brain argues quite possibly Max hasn't written because she hasn't yet found Julien. Annie wants to believe this, but the thought of trouble has created a stumbling block.

When Oliver pops his head into the apothecary to say he is heading upstairs to bed, he sees the worried look on her face.

"I'm certain Max is fine," he says and takes her hand in his. "If anything was wrong you'd be the first person she'd call."

"That's true," Annie says. "But…"

"But nothing." Oliver smiles. "Max is fine." He says this definitively as if it is something he is absolutely certain of.

Annie reluctantly turns off the phone, but even as she trudges up the stairs she can't close down the niggling worry that has settled inside her head.

APARTMENT ON RUE RACINE

When the shouting starts it is so loud that Madame Chastain, the woman in the downstairs apartment, takes a broomstick and bangs against the ceiling.

"Keep it up, and I'm calling the police!" she hollers.

"Drop dead you, old biddy!" Brigitte yells back.

Brigitte is a tiny thing, barely five feet tall and less than one hundred pounds, but she isn't afraid of the devil. Nor is she afraid of either Madame Chastain or Julien.

"Keep your voice down!" Julien shouts, even though his is every bit as loud as hers. He has no fear of Brigitte, but twice the building manager has warned that if the rowdiness continues he will set them and their belongings out on the street. This is something Julien does not want to happen. The rent for this apartment is cheap, and there are three different doorways by which he can leave the building. Right now this is merely a convenience, but given Brigitte's lack of discretion it could one day become a necessity.

She is a liability, but she is also an asset. Her small fingers are so quick and light they can pluck a watch from a wrist before a single second ticks by. She looks harmless, but she can steal a wallet and smile at the same time.

Julien is certain of this. He lowers his voice slightly.

"You saw my signal," he says. "You should have backed off."

Brigitte's mouth curls in a sneer. "Why? Because she's some babe you used to bang?"

"I had feelings for her—"

Brigitte raises her voice three octaves. "Oh, so you had *feelings.* Isn't that special!"

Julien turns away. "It's not something you'd understand," he grumbles.

When he walks into the bedroom, she follows close at his heels.

"And what about me?!" she screams. "I don't have feelings? You think I didn't see you looking at her with those moon eyes?"

"I was surprised to see her, that's all. I didn't expect—"

"You think I'm stupid or something?"

Julien has heard her ask this same question a thousand times before, and he knows there is no good answer. Regardless of what he says, she will come at him tooth and nail.

"No," he says wearily, "I don't think—"

"You're damn right!" she snaps. "I saw you whispering. What'd you say?" Before he has time to answer she screams, "What?" Her voice is so loud it rattles the windowpane.

Madame Chastain again bangs on the ceiling, this time harder.

"I said I was sorry." His voice is now lower, higher than a normal speaking voice perhaps, but considerably lower than hers.

Giving Madame Chastain's banging no notice, Brigitte yells, "Sorry? Sorry about what?"

When he doesn't answer, she grabs an ashtray from the dresser and hurls it at his head. He ducks, but when it hits the bedroom wall it gouges a hole in the plaster then clatters to the floor.

"Liar!"

In the year they have been together, Julien has learned that when Brigitte is in these moods there is no placating her. The best he can do is ride out the storm. On the outside she is willful and strong, but inside she is frail and damaged.

After she is done throwing things there will be tears, and after the tears lovemaking. This is how it has been from the start. Violence and passion; it is what brought them together and what keeps them so.

Even now Brigitte's eyes are filling with water. "You said you'd meet her, didn't you?"

"Of course not."

"Liar! I heard you say it!" Brigitte turns her back to Julien and faces the wall. It irks her to be so weak-willed, yet the tears are something she cannot prevent. She can often hide them but almost never prevent them.

"I didn't mean it," he replies. "I just didn't know what else to say."

Brigitte's voice is softer now, raspy sounding, with a touch of bitterness.

"Why?" she asks. "Why is this one so special?"

Julien hears the throatiness of her question and knows it is time.

"She's not special," he says, then crosses the room and wraps his arms around her narrow little shoulders. "You know you're the one," he whispers.

She gives no answer, so he whirls her around to face him and brings his mouth down hard upon hers. When his hands drop down to lift her buttocks into his body, she wraps her skinny little legs around him and they tumble into the bed.

LONG AFTER THEY HAVE FINISHED making love, Julien lies there staring up at the ceiling. He spoke the truth when he said seeing Maxine was a shock, but he didn't mention that ever since that moment it's been impossible to get her out of his head.

BRIGITTE

Afterward we made love as we always do. First there is fighting, and when I no longer have a stomach for it I fall to tears. Then he comes to me and soothes my sorrow with the passion of his lovemaking. I know I am a stupid woman for letting it be so, but this is how it has always been.

Except this night was different.

He was as he always is, running his hands across my body and whispering his words in my ear, but the hunger of passion was missing. Even at the moment of climax I could feel him thinking about that woman. He was seeing her, not me.

When he rolled back I pretended to sleep, but he didn't even pretend. He just lay there with me in his arms and her on his mind.

Beneath our bed there is a suitcase where we keep the things we will sell. He tossed her phone in with all the others. He did it in an obvious way; a show to prove she meant nothing. But I know Julien as well as he knows me. We are two of a kind. He plans to wait until I am no longer watching and then he will take back her phone, perhaps return it so he can again see her. I can't let that happen.

I am faster than he is and possibly more clever. When he looks for those things, he won't find them.

Last night believing me asleep, he went to the bathroom and in those few moments I grabbed her phone from the suitcase and shoved it between the mattress and spring of our bed. The wallet is already gone. Before we were halfway home I removed the cash and dropped it in a trashcan. When there is an opportunity I will get rid of the phone also. I will take it down to the quay and heave it into the middle of the Seine.

He will look for it; I know he will. I saw the longing in his eyes. He wants her so he will do something to please her, just as he makes love to please me.

When he discovers the phone is not there, he will know I have taken it. But he will say nothing, because to question its absence is to admit he has gone looking for it. This is the pretend world we exist in.

Nothing is really ours. Not the wallets and phones in the suitcase, not the names we use, not even the words of love that pass between us.

It is all stolen. Everything in this apartment belongs to someone else. This is true even of Julien. He is not mine; he belongs to someone else.

The Traveler's Tea

It is after midnight when Max arrives back at the hotel and climbs into bed. She is weary, but given the mix of thoughts running through her head it is impossible to find sleep. For over an hour she tosses and turns lying first on her right side and then her left, scrunching the pillow into a ball then flattening it. Nothing works. Finally she fluffs the pillow, drops her head onto it and lies on her back staring up at the ceiling.

The window is cracked open ever so slightly, a narrow slit that allows the cool night air to drift in. With it come the sounds of the street: the grumble of motorbikes, the bark of a dog, bits of conversation, footsteps. These sounds never change; even now they are as they were then.

It matters not whether her eyes are open or closed, she still sees Julien with tears in his eyes. It was obvious he remembered. But if so, then why did he not come tonight? Did she misread his intent of the café? But if not the Café du Marche then where? Perhaps one of the small cafés on Boulevard Saint Germain? Or the dimly lit restaurant on Grenelle? They'd had good times in every one of those places, but was one more meaningful to him? Did he have a special connection to another café and she'd simply failed to see it? She has seen Julien and he has recognized her, but still there are only questions. The answers are as elusive as Julien himself.

She thinks back to the day they parted. It was with the promise that Julien would soon follow. Walking through the airport complex he'd tightened his arm around her, and she'd felt the hardness of his hipbone nestled into the fleshiness of her waist. He held her close until that last moment when she'd stepped into the security clearance line. Before she moved to the line he'd pulled her body into his, and she'd felt the rapid beat of his heart. Even now she can feel the warmth of his breath in her ear as he whispered his words of love.

It was a long goodbye; long and painful.

Although leaving him was like leaving an arm or leg behind, she'd responded with a light-hearted laugh.

"It won't be long," she'd said. And at the time she'd believed it.

When there was no email, no text, no phone call, not even a response to the letters she'd sent, she held on to her belief that in time he would come. At night when loneliness covered her like a blanket of ice, she drew on the memory of how he'd stayed and watched long after she'd passed through the security line. When she turned off toward Gate 133 he was still standing there, and even though he appeared as little more than a speck she'd seen him raise his arm and wave one last goodbye.

Can a moment such as that ever be forgotten?

This morning Julien had made no mention of any of these things; he'd said only, "I'm sorry."

I'm sorry. Such a meaningless statement.

Max closes her eyes and remembers how her daddy spoke the exact same words the day he packed his suitcase and walked out. Like Julien he'd given no explanation, only a feeble "I'm sorry." He made no mention of Doreen or the baby she'd borne him. He'd given no comfort to her mama when she collapsed into a crumpled heap of tears. He'd said nothing about moving to another state where he'd see Max once a year. Maybe. And not every year.

IT IS THE WEE HOURS of morning when the sounds of the street fade away and Max's exhaustion takes over. Sleep comes but it is fitful, fraught with images that are mixed up and out of place. Mama, Daddy, Julien, Doreen, the waif, Celeste, the Café du Marche waiter. At times she is a teenager; then it is yesterday and she is on the ground with milkshake covering her face. Angry expressions come and go; they move from one person to another. None of it makes sense. There is no story, just faces, twisted and cut into zigzag shapes like mismatched pieces of different puzzles.

ALTHOUGH SHE HAS SLEPT ONLY a few hours, Max is awake at first light. She has much to do this day, and none of it particularly pleasant.

She does one last search of the room, hoping perhaps her wallet and phone have fallen to the floor of the closet or behind the headboard. After she has poked in every last corner and checked the drawers, she empties her tote bag onto the bed and searches through the clutter one last time. Still nothing. Although there is no logic to it, she checks the pockets of her jacket, jeans and trousers. In the end the only thing she comes up with is another five-euro coin and the business card Claude Barrington gave her on the plane. She places the card on the nightstand then wearily trudges in to shower and start the day.

HER FIRST STOP IS AT the hotel desk.

"I've lost my wallet and phone," she tells the clerk. "Could you check and see if perhaps someone has turned them in?"

He pulls a large cardboard box from beneath the counter and begins to rummage through the contents. He lifts out a pair of glasses, a book, a scarf and a sweater.

As he continues to search, Max says, "It's an iPhone with a pink case. The wallet is pink also with a zipper pouch on top."

By then he has reached the bottom of the box. He ruefully shakes his head. "Sorry, mademoiselle. Your things are not here."

He suggests she check her room, and she replies that she has already done so.

"Thoroughly," she adds.

WHEN MAX STEPS OUT ONTO the street the sky is as gray as she is feeling, but at least there is no rain. She starts walking, following the same path she took yesterday. She crosses the street in the same spot, hugs the buildings as she did before and heads for the Petit Pontoise. As she walks she keeps her eyes to the ground, looking left and right, stopping to check beneath the wastebasket at the corner of Rue Monge.

The Petit Pontoise is considerably more crowded than yesterday. Despite the gray skies, there are even a few patrons sitting at the outdoor tables.

Max goes inside and waits to speak to the owner. He carries a tray of coffees outside then returns to Max.

"Oui, mademoiselle?"

She again explains that she has lost her phone and wallet and was hoping perhaps someone had found them and turned them in.

He shakes his head. "Non," he says sympathetically.

"Oh." Max sighs, and the weight of her disappointment is palpable.

"Please, sit, rest a moment," he says and motions to a small table toward the back. "Let me bring you a coffee."

Max welcomes this slight bit of friendship. "No coffee, but I have a special tea I'd like to drink. So if I might have a cup of boiling water..."

"Oui, oui." He pulls the chair out for her, and when she sits he scurries back to the kitchen.

Once she is settled at the table, Max pulls the small box from her bag and opens it. Inside is the silver infuser and a chiffon bag of crushed leaves. Although she has no idea what is in this mix, she trusts Annie and believes in the magic of her teas.

When the shop owner returns, he has a pot of steaming water and a plate with two small croissants.

"No charge," he says and sets them on the table.

Using the small coffee spoon Max scoops a portion of the mix from the bag, fills the infuser, drops it into the cup and then pours the hot water over it.

As she waits for the tea to steep, she catches the fragrance of something familiar. A flower perhaps? No, not a flower; something sweeter. Sugar cane maybe, but she has never been to a field of sugar cane so how could it be familiar? After six minutes, she lifts the infuser from the cup, sets it aside and takes a sip of the tea.

She has added no sugar, yet it is sweet. Suddenly she feels hungry and less miserable. She finishes the first cup then brews a second. While she waits, she eats both croissants. They also have a certain sweetness to them.

As she lingers over the second cup, Max glances out the front window and sees sunlight splashed across the sidewalk.

THE MEMORY PICTURE

After the last drop of tea is gone Max dries the infuser, replaces it in the box and tucks it back into her bag. She leaves the bistro and continues following yesterday's path. Carefully crossing on the same side of the bridge, she makes her way to the front entrance of Notre Dame. Inside she stops for a moment, dips her fingers in the holy water, then touches her hand to her forehead, chest and shoulders in a sign of the cross.

There is only a scattering of people in the sanctuary, so she slides into the same pew she sat in yesterday. She leans forward, says a brief prayer and searches the floor in and around where she is sitting. She finds a two-euro coin lying on the floor and picks it up. There is no way of knowing who it belongs to, so she pockets it.

When she leaves the cathedral the day has grown warm, and the sun is full and bright. Turning onto Quai Tournelle, she feels a nervous flutter pass through her stomach. She slows her steps as she walks the next three blocks. Once she reaches the spot where it happened, she stands perfectly still and tries to recreate the image of all that took place.

She pictures the boy. He is on a skateboard, a yellow

skateboard. She moves from the center of the walkway and stands alongside the stone wall. Again she calls to mind the image of yesterday. This time there are passersby wrapped in ponchos and hooded raincoats. Despite the gray drizzle that clouded the air, it is now easier to envision the boy. He is older than she thought. A small man, not a boy. He zigs left and pushes off speeding up as he races toward her. As he lifts his arm to throw the milkshake, she sees his face.

It is familiar. Someone she knows or has seen somewhere before. A student from the university? She pictures him sitting in the lecture hall or at a table in the library, but neither is right. Then it comes to her. She can see him laughing and climbing astride a motorcycle. He is a friend of Julien.

Max gasps. "Oh my God!"

The words of the waiter come back to her. *One of them creates a diversion, and his accomplice picks your pocket or steals your bag.*

The images are now vivid and real. She feels Julien's arms lift her and sees the girl pick up her bag and hook it over her arm. Max remembers the look of surprise on Julien's face, and she grows teary. Her legs start to tremble and her heart begins beating fast, too fast.

Bracing herself against the wall, she turns away and looks down at the Seine as a riverboat passes by. Taking deep breaths, she waits for her heart to calm itself. A steady stream of tears rolls down her face as she comes to realize the truth of what happened. They were working together: Julien, the man on the skateboard and the girl. It was no accident. It was planned. To Julien she was just another unsuspecting tourist until he looked into her face.

It is the red scarf all over again. The scarf was never truly a gift of love; it was Julien's way of proving he is clever enough to take what he wants from life. He is a man who gives nothing; he only takes. There is no other way to say it; he is a thief.

Fool...believe their lies, and you will fall in love with another one who is just like your daddy!

Max pulls a tissue from her bag and dries her eyes.

"No, Mama, I won't," she mumbles resolutely. She pulls the scarf from her throat and drops it into a trashcan. It flutters down, but one corner catches on the rim of the can and hangs there. It is like her love, a thing that doesn't know how to let go.

FOR THE BETTER PART OF an hour Max remains there looking down at the river, watching boats pass by and trying to piece together her memories of Paris.

So much happened that year. It wasn't just Julien. He came in the winter, but in those few months before him she'd learned to love the city. She'd delighted in studying the old buildings and sitting in front of a single painting for hours on end. She'd walked through the museums and monuments of the Invalides until she could hear the decades-old scratching of pens as wounded soldiers wrote letters to their sweethearts. At the Sainte Genevieve Library she'd discovered an ability to hear the whispered secrets of books and feel the wisdom of years in their yellowed pages. She'd tasted chocolate so sweet it lingered on her tongue for hours and drank wine that made her senses reel. Then she met Julien.

He was a figure so commanding he filled her vision, blocked out everything else and caused her to lose sight of the things she loved. He beckoned and she followed. Willingly. Blindly. Foolishly.

Max reminds herself that Paris was Paris when there was no Julien. To rid herself of his memory, she has only to rediscover what came before him.

She will find those memories and will not allow herself to die of a broken heart as her mama did. But first there are things she must do.

MAX PUSHES THROUGH THE HEAVY glass door, crosses the room and steps to the window.

"I'd like to report a robbery," she says.

The uniformed officer looks up and asks, "Anyone injured?"

She hesitates a moment then shakes her head. "No," she answers, but this is somewhat of a lie. She is injured; just not in a way that is visible.

"You'll have to file a report," the officer says. "English or French?"

"English," Max replies.

He pulls a complaint form from his desk and hands it to her. "You can do it over there." He points to the counter on the far wall.

It is a double-sided form with questions about where, when and how the robbery occurred. She answers these questions then adds a detailed description of the three people involved: Julien, the girl and the man on the skateboard.

After looking her answers over one last time, she returns to the counter and hands the officer the form.

"Merci." He gives a nod as if to dismiss her, and without even glancing at the report he places it in a tray with several others.

"That's it?" Max says. "That's all you're going to do?"

"The theft will be reported," he says. "Standard procedure."

"Isn't someone going to try to find and arrest them?"

"If we apprehend them with your possessions, yes, we will arrest them. But to find a pickpocket in Paris would take an army of men, and even then..." He rolls his eyes as if such a thought is inconceivable.

"I'll give you this one's name!"

Startled, the officer reaches over, retrieves Max's report and reads through what she has written. "You know the man who threw the milkshake on you?"

"Not him," Max says, "the other one. The one with the girl."

The officer eyes her suspiciously. "And how exactly do you know this man?"

"At one time we were friends, close friends..."

"Ah, so then this alleged robbery is because of a lover's quarrel?"

Max notices that he now calls it an *alleged* robbery.

"No," she says indignantly. "I haven't seen or heard from him in over three years." She explains how the hood of her poncho was obscuring her face.

"I'm positive he didn't realize who I was until it was too late; his friend had already thrown the milkshake."

The officer gives a weary nod. "Okay, give me the name."

"Julien Marceau."

"Address?"

Max shrugs. "I have no idea."

Again he rolls his eyes. "We'll do what we can."

WHEN MAX LEAVES THE STATION he again drops her report on the tray with the others.

"A lover's quarrel for sure," he says with a groan and doesn't bother to make note of the name she has given.

MAX

I went to the police station because I thought I'd need a copy of the robbery report to get a replacement credit card. I never planned to give them Julien's name; it just happened. When that policeman all but told me they were going to do nothing, I couldn't stand the unfairness of it.

Julien is a thief. He not only stole my wallet and phone, he stole three years of my life. Even if I could forgive him for stealing my wallet, I can't forgive him for stealing those years. All he had to do was send an email and say we were a mistake. Yes, I would have been heartbroken, but I would have eventually gotten over it and moved on. Instead I believed in him. I believed something terrible had happened, something that prevented him from calling me or reaching out. Looking back I can see how totally stupid that was, but I didn't see it then.

I wish I could tell you I'm completely over Julien, but the sad truth is that even now there is a small part of my heart that still loves him. Maybe not Julien himself, but the memory of him. You can't love someone for all this time and then forget him in a single heartbeat. It takes time.

My plane ticket is non-refundable. I can't exchange it, so to leave now I'd have to buy another ticket. That would cost almost a thousand dollars. I'm not ready to spend that kind of money, and besides going home because of what happened is the same as admitting defeat. No way am I doing that.

I've decided to stay in Paris until next Sunday. I promised Annie that no matter what happened I would return home better off than I was, and I intend to do it. Before Julien and I became us, there was a me. Right now it's that me I need to find.

I'm going to try to rediscover the things that once made me happy; a "before Julien" kind of happy. I know it won't be the same. Nothing ever is. But hopefully I can replace some painful memories with better ones. At least it's something to strive for.

Yes, it's sad to be here alone, but that's how life is. A heart can't learn to heal until it knows it's been broken.

Moving On

It is almost four o'clock when Max arrives back at the hotel that Monday afternoon. She calls the American embassy. The telephone rings sixteen times before it is answered. Finally a recording clicks on and the voice says, "If your passport has been lost, stolen or mutilated and your travel plans are not imminent, the U.S. Embassy can accept your application for a new passport by appointment only. To schedule an appointment, press one."

She continues to listen as the voice rattles on. "If this is an emergency involving the death, arrest, illness or abduction in progress of an American citizen, press two. For all other inquiries, please visit the embassy's website at France-dot-U-S-embassy-dot-gov."

With a sigh of disappointment Max hangs up the phone. Since her situation is none of those listed, she is certain that help from the embassy will not come in time to salvage what she has left of this vacation.

AGAIN SHE COUNTS THE COINS in the side pocket. Seventeen euros. Enough for a couple of sandwiches and a coffee or two. Not enough to live on for another six days. The hotel is covered because the clerk zapped her credit card the day she arrived, but still there is food, train fare back to the airport and...

Max is not sure what else she will need, nor does she know where to turn for help. She sits on the side of the bed trying to recall the names of classmates, but it was over three years ago and many of her friends were foreigners just as she was.

Greta Mulberg comes to mind, a girl with a long switch of blonde hair worn clipped to the top of her head. But Greta was from Holland. Jeff Franklin, another friend from somewhere in the Midwest. Then she remembers Louis Pointier, a language student who was at one time fond of her. He came from a small town outside of Paris. Max racks her brain trying to remember the name of the town. Finally it comes to her: Gouvieux.

She thinks back on the evenings spent with these friends, usually in an inexpensive café with a shared bottle of wine and sandwiches of meat and cheese. It was Louis who often paid the check. Like her most students were scraping by on a meager allowance, but not Louis. He always had money in his pocket and petrol for his motorbike.

Twice Max had gone to dinner with him; both times he had taken her to a fancy restaurant with candles and menus offering countless delicacies. That was before Julien. The last time he asked her out, she told him of Julien and he'd not asked again. Even so, he would remember her. She was a friend.

She will call him, and they will chat about old times; then when she explains her situation he will gladly lend her the money she needs. Perhaps he will ask if they can once more have dinner together. This is a pleasant thought.

She calls information and asks for the number. There is no listing for Louis Pointier. She inquires about a listing with another first name. It's possible Louis moved to a different town, in which case she'll ask the family for his telephone number. There are a few moments of silence; then the operator says there is no listing for any Pointier in the town of Gouvieux. Max switches the spelling of Pointier, leaving out the first "i". When that produces nothing she then tries reversing the "e" and "i", but still there is no listing. When there is nothing left to try, she thanks the operator and hangs up.

It is then she notices the business card laying on the nightstand.

Claude Barrington, President, Barrington Enterprises, Richmond, Virginia.

A fellow traveler, but little more than a passing acquaintance. Still, they'd had a lovely conversation, and he'd definitely shown an interest in her until she mentioned Julien. Claude Barrington is here in Paris. Visiting a friend or staying with a friend? She remembers the charm of his smile and tries to recall the words of their conversation.

Suddenly it comes to her.

"Hotel Baltimore!" she shouts and reaches for the telephone.

"Bonjour, Hotel Baltimore," a voice says, "how may I help you?"

"I'd like to speak to—" Max stops and hangs up.

It is a ridiculous thought, to telephone someone and ask to borrow money after such a casual meeting. The probability is he would simply hang up or say a flat out no. It would be far better to go there in person, ask to speak with him, chat for a while and then tell him of her predicament. She thinks on how he'd so courteously bought her a drink even after her mention of Julien. He was obviously a gentleman, and in a face-to-face meeting it is unlikely he'll refuse to help.

Max checks her reflection in the mirror. Her mascara is streaked down the left side of her face, her lips dry and crackled. She peels off her clothes and steps into the shower.

Forty-five minutes later she leaves the hotel wearing pointy-toed high heels, her good black trousers and lip gloss the same shade of pink as her sweater.

CLEVER GIRL

On Monday morning Julien pretends to be asleep until he feels Brigitte turn on her back and stretch her arms. He waits, knowing that in less than a minute she will lift herself from the bed and head for the bathroom. When he hears the click of the shower door, he climbs from bed and pulls out the suitcase. He expects the pink phone to be right on top, but it is not. There is only the usual mix of black phones, brown wallets and loose credit cards.

"What the hell…" he grumbles. Pushing the top layer aside, he rummages through the remainder of their collection. Max's phone is not there. When the shower stops he hurriedly snaps the suitcase shut and slides it back under the bed.

Last night Brigitte's jealousy bristled like the quills of a porcupine, and he knew what was in her mind. Now the phone is gone, and he has no one to blame but himself. There must have been a moment when he turned away, a split second when he blinked and she snatched it from beneath his nose.

He knows she is lightning fast and will pocket whatever she wants. He should have been more careful. He should have taken the phone from the suitcase and hidden it elsewhere. Now it is too late.

Brigitte pads into the bedroom, her hair trailing drips of water down her back. Her mouth is pulled into a pout, and the anger of last night is still in her eyes.

"Finally awake?" she says. "You certainly slept long enough." The words are harmless, but there is an icy edge to them.

Julien pretends not to notice. *She is a fox*, he thinks, *but new at the game*. He has much more experience.

"So, what would you like to do today?" he asks lazily. Before she has time to answer he adds that he is thinking they should gather the merchandise they have and take it to the buyer.

"We could use the money," he says.

"Oh, really?" She turns with a suspicious glare. "Strange, because two days ago your pockets were full."

"Money goes." He gives a casual shrug. "A bit here, a bit there…"

Brigitte knows him as well as she knows herself, and his words are a touch too nonchalant. When they take the phones to the buyer Julien is usually edgy and in a foul mood. He doesn't like dealing with the old man who is arrogant and a ruthless negotiator; in the end, though, the buyer pays cash and asks no questions.

"Why him, and why now?" she asks.

"I told you, we need the money."

She knows he has looked for the girl's phone and not found it.

"You've been at the suitcase, haven't you?" she says sarcastically. "And now you think I'll tell you where her phone is."

He looks at her with a raised eyebrow and puzzled expression. "Where whose phone is?"

"You know who," she snaps. "The girl from yesterday!"

"Oh," Julien laughs. "I'd forgotten about that." His laugh is lighthearted and almost believable.

He waits for her reaction. When the hard set of her jaw begins to soften he says, "I don't care about her phone. Do as you want with it. Keep it or take it to the buyer, but remove the pink case. It's too identifiable, and I don't want it traced back to us."

For a moment Brigitte wonders if perhaps this time he is telling the truth. Maybe she is wrong; maybe the woman means nothing to him. She wants to believe this but cannot forget the look in his eyes.

"Don't worry," she says, "I've already removed the case. I threw it in the trash bin last night."

He says nothing but in the silence she can sense his thoughts; he is not nearly as clever as he thinks.

"Afterward I put her phone back in the suitcase," she says.

Julien looks at her but still says nothing. She is a good liar, so it is impossible to know whether this is true. He tries to remember if she carried trash to the bin last night but cannot.

He gives her a tight little smile and moves back to his earlier question. "So, what would you like to do today?"

"You said you wanted to take the phones to the buyer."

"Well, if you'd rather not..."

"No, if it is as you say and we need the money, then—"

"Let me check," he replies.

He goes to the closet, moves the carton of books aside and lifts the loose floorboard. Beneath the floorboard there is a small metal box. This is where the money is kept. He opens the box and makes a show of counting the money.

"One thousand one hundred and sixty euros." He smiles. "More than I thought."

"Good," Brigitte answers. She waits to hear what he will say now.

He gives her a flirtatious smile; it is a smile that almost assures he will get his way.

"For now we have enough," he says, "so the buyer can wait. Today we will treat ourselves to an afternoon at the Tulleries and dinner at the café."

A look of sorrow slides across Brigitte's face. "Fine."

Her answer is flat and weighted with resentment, but Julien doesn't notice. His thoughts are on the phones in the suitcase. Max's phone is in with all the others. He has only to wait until Brigitte is out, and then he will go through them one by one. There is sure to be something that will let him know which one is hers. A picture perhaps or a message.

BRIGITTE

J ulien is like a pane of glass. I see inside his thoughts even when he
thinks he has hidden them. He speaks as though he cares nothing
for this woman, but he is a poor liar. The truth is all over him,
obvious as the nose on his face.

He believes her phone is with the others, and when my back is turned
he will search the suitcase looking to find it. This morning when I asked
if he still wanted to take the phones to the buyer, I prayed he would
answer yes but he didn't. I fear she is a disease in his blood, just as he is a
disease in mine.

You might wonder why I would let myself love a man such as this,
but the truth is I have no choice. He owns me. He took my soul with
gentle promises and a passion as hot as the fires of hell.

It is not always angry words and trickery. There are times when it is
good between us, times when he covers me with kisses and makes love as
if I am the only woman in the world. When he does this, I soak it up like
a sugary poison. I know it will one day destroy me, but still I hunger for
the sweetness of it.

His other dalliances have been short-lived. A night here, a night
there, but always he comes back to me. I am afraid this woman is

different. If he goes to her he may never return, and I will be back on the street where I was when he found me.

I am not going to let that happen.

THE FIRST MESSAGE

Annie has read and reread Max's message a dozen or more times, yet she cannot dismiss the troubling premonition that has settled in her head. Throughout the night she tossed and turned, unable to sleep, unable to rid herself of the thought that her friend is in trouble. Were this a year ago she might have felt differently, but with all that has happened she knows such a premonition can easily as not be a warning.

For most of the night she visualized the catastrophes that could have taken place. Then when the earliest streaks of pink filtered into the sky she finally decided the most likely problem is Julien. Max has not yet found Julien. That has to be it. She hasn't found Julien, so she simply isn't ready to talk.

Once this decision is settled in her mind, Annie gives a sigh of relief then closes her eyes and drifts off to sleep.

WHEN OLIVER WAKES AT SEVEN o'clock Monday morning, she is sleeping soundly. During the night he sensed her restlessness, so he quietly scoots from the bed without disturbing her. At eight-thirty when he is ready to leave for the courthouse, he jots a quick note and places it on the nightstand beside the bed.

The long night has taken its toll on Annie, and she sleeps until almost ten. When she finally wakes it is because of the harsh cry of the blackbird sitting on the window ledge. It is a sound that pierces her ears like a shrill whistle. She climbs from the bed, goes to the window and raps on the pane.

"Shoo," she says. "Shoo, get out of here."

The bird flaps its wings and stays put.

Annie turns back toward the bed, but before she can climb into it the bird resumes its raucous cawing.

Suddenly Annie snaps fully awake. She remembers her thoughts of last night and jumps to the conclusion that the black bird is a sign. Without bothering to pull on a bathrobe, she darts down the stairs and grabs her cell phone.

A swell of anxiety has already settled in her chest, and it grows larger as she waits for the phone to load. "Come on, come on…" she says impatiently.

Once the phone is loaded she clicks on messages. There is nothing new.

"I thought by now…"

Annie lays the phone on the kitchen table and lights a fire beneath the teakettle. She brews a cup of dandelion tea and then taps in a note to Max.

> I'm concerned I haven't heard from you. Is everything OK? Don't be disappointed if you don't find Julien. Sometimes these things happen for the best. Trust your heart and you'll find a truer love. Be sure to message me when you get this. I'm worried. Love, Annie

She rereads the message then clicks send. It is 10:17AM in Burnsville.

Moments later the message arrives on Max's phone. A muffled beep comes from beneath the mattress, but there is no one around to hear it. At 4:17 Julien is walking through the gardens of Tulleries with Brigitte.

◦◦◦

TEN MINUTES AFTER SHE HAS sent the message, the telephone in Annie's hallway rings. She hurriedly lifts the receiver and says, "Max?"

Ophelia laughs. "Sorry, it's only me."

There is a momentary sigh of disappointment; then Annie laughs. "*Only* you? There's nobody more special than you."

Before they go any further Ophelia asks, "Have you been drinking that dandelion tea from the top shelf?"

"Why, yes I have," Annie answers. "Just this morning. I was feeling—"

"I knew it!" Ophelia cuts in. "I just made myself a cup of that tea, and before I'd had two sips a thought came into my head saying call Annie right now."

"Get out!"

"I swear. It was clear as day."

Annie laughs. "Well, I have been a bit worried about Max."

"I know," Ophelia says. "That's why I thought tonight would be a good night for me to come to dinner; that is, if you'll have me."

"Of course we'll have you. We'd be delighted. Oliver can pick you up on the way home from the courthouse."

"Good." Ophelia hesitates then adds, "I'll bring my toothbrush and nightie, because I might be staying over."

"That would be lovely," Annie says. "Now that the weather's

turned nice and warm, we can sit out on the porch and—"

"We'll see," Ophelia says.

She knows a storm is coming. She knows by the feeling that has settled into her bones. It will be a storm worse than the one that blew through the day Edward died. She doesn't mention this to Annie because hopefully she is wrong, but if not she needs to be there at Memory House. That is where it all began and where it will one day end.

As she sits at the table sipping the last of her tea, Ophelia folds her hands in her lap and prays.

"Please, Lord," she says. "Let it not be tonight."

THE THREE OF THEM, ANNIE, Oliver and Ophelia, are seated at the kitchen table when the first crack of thunder comes. There is no warning, just a flash of light zigzagging across the sky. Then a boom rattles the walls of the house.

"Good grief," Annie exclaims. "Where did that come from?"

Within minutes it sounds like a war is being waged overhead. The single clap of thunder is followed by another and then yet another. One minute the sky is ablaze with lightning; the next it is black as the bottom of a mine. Before the thunder stops, the wind starts. It comes with such force the teacups on the cupboard shelf rattle, and a small vinegar pitcher bounces off the counter and crashes onto the floor.

Ophelia's lips are moving, but there is no sound. She is silently repeating the prayer that has been on her tongue all afternoon. She knew this was coming, but what disasters it will leave behind she does not know.

"I think we should wait this one out down in the basement," Oliver says.

Annie nods. Her face is pale, and her eyelids flutter nervously. She stands, lifts the leftover platter of chicken and slides it into the refrigerator. Lighting the flame beneath the teakettle, she says, "I'll make a pot of tea to bring with us."

"No time," Ophelia says. She switches the burner off. "We have to go now." Her voice is tight and edgy.

Oliver grabs Annie's hand and pulls her toward the cellar. Ophelia is right behind. As they leave the kitchen, he reaches into the top drawer and grabs a flashlight. On the back side of the hallway is the door that leads to the basement. He snaps on the light and starts down the steps. Ophelia is the last one to enter; as she passes through the door she closes it behind her.

Annie has been down here countless times but never considered it a storm shelter. Along the walls are shelves where she stores canisters of herbs and flowers pulled from the garden. In back of the canisters are glass jars of clover honey, cherry jam and dilly beans. On the bottom shelf there are gallon jugs of water and a cardboard box that contains a never-before-used lantern. Ophelia placed those there over a decade ago. She has always known this time would come.

There are no windows in the basement, yet they can still hear the howl of wind and hammering of rain. Days earlier the weather turned warm. This is the season for summer showers, yet the pounding against the house has the sound of something far worse.

"I think that's hail," Oliver says.

Ophelia knows he is right.

Several booms come in rapid succession. Before the last one has died away there is a thundering thud, and the house shudders. The sound of shattering glass comes from upstairs.

In her mind's eye Ophelia can see the tall pine on the south side of the house has crashed through the overhang of the dining room window.

Moments later the basement light dims then goes black.

HOTEL BALTIMORE

The metro would be faster, but since she has only seventeen euros and no guarantee of Claude Barrington's generosity Max walks. Wearing high heels slows her pace, but there is plenty of time. She will be there by six-thirty, seven at the latest.

Taking a shortcut over to Saint Germain Boulevard she turns west, then onto Quai d'Orsay and across the George V Bridge. Once on the Right Bank, it is only a twenty-minute walk. Her stomach grumbles as she passes the cluster of restaurants in the Trocadero Circle. She wonders if perhaps Claude will suggest dinner and smiles at the thought of sitting across from him at one of the quaint outdoor cafés. From the circle she turns right onto Kiebler Avenue. The Hotel Baltimore is only five blocks down. She can already see the Arc d' Triomphe.

Max has passed the hotel a number of times but never been inside. It's a large building that sits on Kiebler Avenue then rounds the corner and takes up a good part of Rue Leo Delibes. From the street it is easy to see the elegance of the interior through the large plate glass windows. Even now it is as intimidating as it was three years ago.

She enters the building and crosses to the front desk.

"I'd like to speak with Monsieur Claude Barrington," she says. "I'm not certain of his room number."

"And your name, mademoiselle?"

"Max," she says, then corrects herself. "Maxine Martinelli." The simplicity of "Max" is somehow inappropriate in such an environment.

"One moment, s'il vous plait," he says then lifts the telephone receiver and punches in a number.

There is a wait that to Max seems interminable. She wonders if on the plane she gave Claude her full name. Perhaps; perhaps not. Even if she did, how likely is it that he will remember a name like Martinelli? Maybe she should have stayed with Max.

The clerk hangs up the receiver and explains that there is no answer in Monsieur Barrington's room.

"Was he expecting you?" he asks.

"Not really," Max replies. "We were both in town, and I thought perhaps…"

"If you care to wait…" He motions to a lounge area scattered with plush leather sofas.

"For a while," she says and walks toward a sofa grouping that looks out onto Kiebler Avenue. She sits in a spot where she can watch the front door. If she sees him coming, she will bounce up and pretend to run into him accidently. Once they start to chat it will be easier to tell him of her predicament.

She glances at her watch, then back to the door.

IT IS AFTER EIGHT O'CLOCK when Max finally decides to leave. This was a foolish idea to start with, she tells herself. Claude Barrington is a stranger. A man she sat next to on the plane. Why would he care about her problems? It's possible that he simply didn't wish to be bothered. Maybe he has been upstairs in his room this whole while, waiting for her to leave, hoping she will go away and take her problems with her.

A feeling of foolishness sweeps over Max. She stands, blinks back the tears and starts toward the door.

A voice comes from behind her. "Max?"

She turns and comes face to face with Andrew Steen, Oliver Doyle's one-time law partner.

"I thought that was you," he says.

"Hi," she says warily. As much as she needs a friend right now, it's difficult to forget the last time she talked about a problem in front of Andrew. It was New Year's Day. She'd spoken of how Brianna said not having an office automatically slotted her in the loser column, and he'd agreed. The thought of it is enough to make her blood boil all over again.

If she were to make a list of people to ask for help Andrew would not even be on the list, or if he were he'd be way below Claude Barrington. But what if she can't connect with the stranger?

Andrew at least knows her. If for no reason other than his friendship with Oliver and Annie, he'd likely lend her enough money to tide her over. It's not as if she'd be asking for a handout; it would be a loan. A loan she'd repay the minute she returns to the U.S.

She pushes back the memory of their last encounter and smiles.

"What are you doing in Paris?" she asks.

"Business," Andrew replies. "I handle Lazar's U.S. interests. And you?"

"It's a long story." She tries to stave off the melancholy she feels, but it's impossible. It's in her voice, in her eyes and stretched across her face.

"Are you okay?" he asks.

If Max didn't know better she'd think he was concerned, but

she knows him and is certain that telling the truth would make her seem even more of a loser than not having an office. She shrugs and repeats, "It's a long story."

"I was on my way to dinner," he says. "Why don't you join me? We can have a drink, and you can tell me this long story."

Max hesitates.

Andrew sees it and remembers their last encounter. She'd decided he was criticizing her before he'd had a chance to explain. He lifts his hands, palms out, an apology for having stepped over the line.

"Of course, if you have somewhere else to go..."

"Actually, I don't," she says. "Dinner sounds good."

He grins. It's a boyish grin that somehow makes her more comfortable about talking to him. When he offers his arm she takes it.

"They have a nice restaurant here at the hotel," he suggests.

"That's fine," she answers. Max has not eaten since the two small croissants early this morning and is famished.

THEY SETTLE AT THE TABLE, and Andrew orders a bottle of wine.

"White okay?" he asks, and she nods.

For a while there is only small talk. He says he arrived this morning and will be here until Thursday; she says she is staying until Sunday. He tells her he is here at the Baltimore; she says she has a room at the Vendome.

"It's a small hotel over in the Latin Quarter," she explains.

"I've never been to that area," he says.

Before she stops to think through her words, Max replies, "I suppose it's kind of low-brow for you." Almost instantly she knows she has said the wrong thing.

A slight wince twitches the corner of Andrew's mouth.

"You're always so damn quick to jump to conclusions," he

says indignantly. "The reason I don't stay down there is because the Lazar offices are two blocks from here. On these Paris trips I fly in, take a cab from the airport, attend business meetings for three or four days, then take a cab back to the airport and fly out."

"I'm sorry," Max says sheepishly. "You're right, I am too quick to jump to conclusions."

They finish the first glass of wine and order dinner. Andrew suggests the veal; he says he dines here often because of its convenience.

"And the food is really great," he adds. Max goes with his recommendation because right now anything would taste good, and she is making an all-out effort to be agreeable.

The conversation starts out stilted, but by the time he pours their second glass of wine it has eased.

"So," he says, "are you ready to tell me this long story you've got?"

Max gives a chagrined smile. "I guess so," she says. Although she cannot bring herself to tell of Julien, she does explain that she has been robbed and now has no phone and no credit cards.

"Do you think maybe you could lend me enough money to make it through next Sunday? I can pay you back the minute—"

"Of course." Andrew reaches into his pocket, pulls out a handful of bills and peels off a half-dozen fifty-euro notes. "This should last a day or two. I can give you more if you need it, but I think you need to cancel your credit card and get a replacement."

"I can't," Max says, "at least not until I get home. The bank phone number, my account number, even the password is all stored in my phone and—"

"What bank do you use?"

"First Richmond."

Andrew checks his watch and grins. "You're in luck. It's only three-fifteen in Virginia, and First Richmond is where I have my business account. I'm on a first-name basis with my rep." He pulls out his phone, scrolls down the list of contacts and taps the bank logo.

Moments later he is talking and laughing with someone called Susan. He explains the situation and asks her to look up Max's account.

"I can vouch for her," he says, "she's right here with me." Before he hangs up, Susan has cancelled Max's old card and is overnighting a new one via FedEx. She's promised it will be in Max's hands by Wednesday.

"You are a miracle worker!" Max laughs, and this time the sound of her laughter is genuine. "How can I ever thank you?"

"Give me a minute or two, and I'm sure I can come up with a few ideas," Andrew says. Then he returns her smile.

MAX

I n a million years I would have never guessed I'd meet Andrew
Steen here in Paris, and it could be two million before I would
have guessed he'd be so nice about helping me out.

Up until last night I thought he was somewhat of a snob. But the
truth is he's just a bit shy. Once he gets started talking he's actually fun.
You know, in a casual sort of way. He's smart too. I was amazed at how
he called the bank and bingo-bongo got me a new credit card.

I felt ridiculous telling him the real reason I came to Paris was to
find Julien, so I said I wanted to be inspired by the architecture. Thinking
back on it I guess that sounded like a pretty lame reason, but it was all I
could come up with at the moment. I was too ashamed to admit
I've wasted three years of my life pining over the same guy who robbed
me.

Okay, maybe it wasn't Julien who actually stuck his hand in my bag
and took those things, but it's still the same thing. He and the girl are a
team, and in my mind one is as guilty as the other. Actually, I feel sort of
sorry for her. My bet is that sooner or later he'll do her just as he's done
me.

Julien gets away with it because he's the kind of guy girls turn
around to look at, so you feel good about being the one he's with. At the

time you're so infatuated with his looks and charm you don't stop to think about the fact that he hasn't got one ounce of character.

Andrew is the total opposite. He's sort of ordinary looking. Cute, but not the kind of cute that makes your eyeballs pop out. His hair is this curly kind of messed up, and he's got nice eyes. He's also got a really sweet smile. It's funny, I never before noticed how genuine his smile is. When I said he was my hero for dealing with the bank as he did, he blushed.

Imagine a guy blushing. Julien could stand naked in the middle of the Champs Elysées and wouldn't blush.

Actually, I thought it was kind of sweet Andrew blushing like that. When I asked if there was some way I could repay his kindness he finally said yes, I could go sightseeing with him. He's been to Paris six times and not once been to the Louvre or the d'Orsay. How can you possibly be in Paris and not visit those museums?

Andrew has a meeting this morning, but he said let's get together this afternoon. Not like a date or anything but just to hang out and do some sightseeing. He suggested the Louvre, but it's closed on Tuesday so we're going to the d'Orsay. I enjoy the d'Orsay more anyway, and I think he will too.

Maybe I'll surprise him and stop by the museum to pick up tickets before we meet. Yeah, that's what I'm going to do. It's kind of a way of repaying him for how nice he's been to me.

Annie is going to die laughing when I tell her about this.

SURVEYING THE DAMAGE

It is the wee hours of Tuesday morning before the wind finally subsides and the sound of things thumping against the house ceases. Annie and Ophelia are lying on the cot, curled together like two fingers of the same hand. Annie, with her arm tucked beneath her stomach, seems to be cradling the unborn child. Oliver paces the floor; he walks to the edge of the circle of light then turns and comes back again. Ophelia's oil lamp is enough to light this small area of the room, but the rest of the basement is in total blackness.

Oliver checks his watch. Two-thirty. He waits and listens for another fifteen minutes then says he is going upstairs to check on the damage. He clicks on the flashlight and starts up the steps.

"Be careful," Annie calls out, but careful of what she doesn't say.

"Don't worry," Oliver replies.

His footsteps are slow and cautious. The howl of the storm was worse than anything he has ever heard, so he is uncertain of what to expect. As soon as he pushes open the basement door he catches the odor of wet earth. Extending his arm in front of him, he swishes the circle of light back and forth to see where it is safe to step and where it is not. In the hallway there is broken glass, and the picture that once hung in the living room is torn apart. The frame lays splintered into sticks of wood.

From here he can see the front door. It is still intact. No damage there. He moves back toward the kitchen and feels water squish beneath his feet. Shining the light toward the dining room, he sees a branch large enough to be considered a tree atop the dining room table. Ophelia's suspicion is correct; the tall pine has come down on the house. Splashes of rain still blow through the broken window.

The branch needs to be cut into pieces and carried out, but it will have to wait until daylight. He continues to the kitchen. In here the air is heavy with the earthy smell of the storm, but there is no damage other than a geranium that has fallen to the floor and broken the pot. He breathes a sigh of relief and crosses to the alcove that leads to the back porch. He tries the door, but it seems to be stuck. He sticks the flashlight in his pocket and tugs at the door until it finally gives way and creaks open.

Something feels wrong. Oliver hesitates before stepping across the threshold. He pulls the flashlight from his pocket and swishes the small circle of light back and forth across where the porch should be, but there is nothing. Not a hanging patch of screen, an overturned table or even a throw pillow.

Impossible, he thinks.

With one hand braced against the inside frame of the door and the flashlight gripped tightly in the other, he sticks his head out the door. The back porch is gone. There are a few loose boards dangling from the side of the house, but everything else has disappeared.

"I can't believe it!" he exclaims.

He pulls back inside and slams the door hard enough for it to remain stuck.

More wary than ever, he continues through the house. Downstairs there is no further damage. The mustiness of the storm is everywhere, but that is little more than an inconvenience compared to the damage of the back porch. The apothecary is the only room that does not have the odor of the storm. It has somehow held on to the sweet fragrances of lavender, ginger and chamomile.

The loft is the only remaining room to check. But seeing the back porch torn loose from the house has unnerved Oliver, and as he starts up the stairs he prays the skylight has not come crashing down.

Taking the steps slowly, he listens for the sound of an unfamiliar creak and tests the sturdiness of each stair before lifting his full weight onto it. At the top of the staircase he pauses for a deep breath then pushes the door open. He is prepared for the worst, but the room is completely intact. He turns the circle of light toward the skylight and sees it covered with debris from the storm but otherwise unharmed.

"A miracle," he mumbles.

After he has gone through the entire house, he returns to the basement to tell Ophelia and Annie of the damage.

"It's safe to come upstairs," he says. "The dining room is in rough shape, but the bedrooms are okay."

"Any other damage?" Annie asks.

Oliver knows the news about the back porch will upset Annie—it is where she sits to crochet and read—but he cannot bring himself to tell her the lie she wants to hear.

"I'm sorry, the back porch is..."

The word "gone" is on the tip of his tongue, but he holds it back. Gone has such a final sound. Being gone is the same as being dead. Instead he says, "Irreparably damaged."

Annie's eyes grow teary. "Irreparably? You mean it can't be fixed?"

He gives a solemn nod. "What was there can't be fixed, but it can be replaced."

Ophelia already knows the porch is gone. She has seen it in her mind's eye, the same as she saw the tall pine come down on the house. She takes Annie's hand in hers and pats it reassuringly.

"The porch was only sticks of wood and patches of screen. It's not something to fret about."

"It's just that we made such beautiful memories out there..."

Annie is remembering the night Oliver came home from the hospital, and her voice is thick with the sound of melancholy.

"And you've still got those," Ophelia reminds her. "The only things lost were bits of wood and screen.

"I know," Annie replies, but the sadness is still there.

In the dark of a moonless night there is no way to assess the damage, so this night Annie and Oliver sleep in one of the downstairs bedrooms with Ophelia across the hall. Although the loft appears unharmed, there is no way to know for certain.

IT FEELS AS THOUGH THEY have barely closed their eyes when the gray light of morning comes. The storm is gone, but the clouds are thick and so low the giant oak disappears into their midst. There is still no electricity, but the gas stove works as does the water heater. After a quick shower, Oliver pulls on jeans and steps outside to access the damage.

It is everywhere. Two trees are down, one of them lying across the driveway. Shingles and pieces of wood are scattered across the yard, and although the wisteria bushes have not been torn from the ground they are flattened and will need to be staked.

It's obvious Oliver will not be going to the courthouse today. When he tries to call he discovers that without electricity the cordless phones are useless. His only hope is the landline in the hallway. He lifts the receiver and after a long wait finally gets a dial tone.

The call goes through, but it rings and rings with no answer. Just as he is about to hang up, there is a "Hello?" on the other end.

"Who's this?" Oliver asks.

"Fred." Fred is the night custodian of the building.

"Oh, hi, Fred. This is Judge Doyle. Is anyone else at the courthouse?"

"No, sir. Everything downtown's closed. The stores, everything. The streetlights ain't even working."

"Has there been any news about what happened?"

"Man on the radio said a storm stalled overhead and there was buncha tornados. Burnsville and Wyattsville got the worst a' it."

"Any fatalities?"

"He ain't said."

Annie has breakfast ready by the time Oliver hangs up. There is no coffee, but there is black tea, bacon, eggs and biscuits. As the three of them sit down to eat, Ophelia says a prayer thanking the Lord that this was not her time. For years she wished only to be reunited with Edward; now she would prefer to wait a bit longer. The thought of being a grandmother is a future she looks forward to.

After seeing the tree that blocks the driveway, Oliver is anxious to get started.

"Do you know if there's a saw or maybe an axe around here?" he asks.

Ophelia nods. "I think there's something in the storage shed."

Oliver woofs down the last piece of bacon then pulls on his rubber boots and tromps out to the shed. There he finds a handsaw and a bone-dry chain saw. Taking a chance on the chain saw, he siphons gas from the tank of his car, fills the reservoir then yanks the starter cord. Nothing. He tries again and then again. On the third pull it starts.

He gives a smile of satisfaction and heads for the tree blocking the driveway.

Annie is now thirty-six weeks along. Oliver's first priority is to clear the drive so if something happens he will be able to get her to the hospital. That is, if the hospital is operational.

Being without news is like being stuck at the bottom of a well. Hopefully the electricity will be back on before the day is out.

OPHELIA

I told Annie the back porch was nothing to worry about, that it was only sticks of wood and pieces of screen, but that was a lie. The porch meant as much to me as it did to her. Maybe more. Every splinter of wood was filled with memories: memories of the nights Edward and I would sit outside looking up at the stars and planning all the things we'd one day do.

Back then I didn't have this gift for seeing how things were going to happen, and perhaps it's better that way. Just because you can see the inevitability of a tragedy doesn't mean you can stop it from happening. God knows if I had the power to change the course of events, Edward would still be here today.

Annie and Oliver are young and just getting started with their life. Before the year is out they'll rebuild the porch and start making new memories. Me, I'm too old for such a thing. I cling to the old memories, the ones that are worn thin and covered with cobwebs. Even though they are old, to me they are as comforting as a flannel bathrobe.

This morning I stepped outside, looked up at where the porch used to be and felt the tears coming to my eyes. There was a little bitty piece of white wood lying on the ground, so I picked it up and held on to it. I knew it was part of the baseboard Edward painted all those years ago.

As I stood there thinking about all that was lost, I started realizing I hadn't lost anything. I still had all my memories. I even had a piece of the baseboard to hold on to.

Looking at that piece of wood in my hand made me think back on something Edward once said. I was fretting over a handkerchief I'd lost and he told me, "Opie, you've got to enjoy what you have and quit worrying about what you've lost. Worry just makes a person crazy and takes away the pleasure of life."

A few minutes later I found three more pieces of that same baseboard, and that's when I knew it was Edward's way of showing me he'd been there all along. He'd been watching over me, the same as he's done for all these years.

THE D'ORSAY

O n Tuesday afternoon Max is waiting in the lobby of the Hotel Baltimore when Andrew comes rushing through the front door.

"Sorry, I'm late," he says. "The meeting ran longer than expected."

"No problem," Max replies, and she means it. Sometime late last night she slid Andrew into the same category as Annie and Ophelia: a friend worth waiting for. A friend with no stigma or expectations attached.

"I only got here fifteen minutes ago," she says.

"Good," he replies. "I'm glad you weren't—"

Without waiting for him to finish she adds, "I stopped at the museum on the way over and got our tickets. It's a two-day museum pass, so if you want to go to the Louvre tomorrow you can."

"Did you also get one for yourself?" he asks.

She nods. "Of course. I love being at the museums. No matter how often I go, it seems new every time. Even if you're looking at the same painting, there's always some detail or unique brush stroke you've missed seeing before. It gives me a bit of a thrill when I find something like that."

The anticipation in her voice is something Andrew has not heard before. He smiles and says, "I'll have the desk call for a taxi."

"No taxi. The metro is faster." She reaches into her pocket. "It's only three stops, and I've already got tickets."

The corner of Andrew's mouth curls. "You're full of surprises, aren't you?"

"Well, now that I've got some money in my pocket, I can afford to be adventuresome." She hesitates then adds, "Thanks to you."

As they descend the station stairs, she hands him a ticket and says, "You've ridden the metro before, haven't you?"

"Afraid not. I told you it's the airport, ho—"

"I know," she teases, "it's the airport, hotel, the client's office, then back to the airport."

She slides her ticket into the turnstile slot and waits for it to pop out, and then he does the same thing. They wait one minute and twenty-six seconds for a train and arrive at the museum shortly before two.

The moment they step inside Andrew says, "Wow, this place is awesome." He is looking up at the rounded glass ceiling of the main hall.

"Beautiful, huh?"

He nods. "I'll say."

"The ceiling is high because this was once a train station. The main platform was right here in this very same spot." She sidles up to Andrew and whispers, "If you close your eyes and listen, you can still hear the sound of trains coming and going from the station."

"Hear what trains?" he asks. Andrew, like Oliver, is a left-brain person. He thinks in terms of logic, and there is none in such a statement.

Max grins. She is a right-brained daydreamer who feels

rhythms, colors and spatial awareness. The memories in this hall are stronger than any Max has ever found. It is where she first discovered the auras that are left behind. On the coldest days of January she could come to this hall and smell the aroma of the roasted chestnuts that street vendors once sold. She cannot begin to count the number of days she sat on the side of the marble stair and did nothing but envision the trains rolling in and out of the station. When she let go of everything else, Max could hear the swish of long skirts as women passed by and feel the courtliness of the men who walked beside them.

She sighs. "I could spend a year in this hallway alone, but since we've got less than four hours let's start on the fifth floor. You'll love the Impressionists gallery."

They take the elevator to the fifth floor then stroll from room to room, admiring the works of the nineteenth-century masters along with paintings just as beautiful but created by lesser known artists.

Stopping in front of Cezanne's *Apples and Oranges*, Max says, "See how he's captured the fullness of summer? This picture makes me hunger for a piece of fruit that beautiful and sweet."

"Yeah," Andrew says. "Me too." But he's looking at Max, not the picture.

They move past *Olympia* and several other Edouard Manet paintings, then stand for several minutes in front of the huge painting depicting Courbet's studio. When they come to Monet's *Blue Water Lilies*, it is Andrew who stops.

"Wow," he says. "I like the mood he created here. You can see it's water lilies, but they seem more ethereal than regular water lilies."

"The water lily paintings are what Monet's famous for. They're supposedly scenes from the garden at his house. I've heard it's beautiful beyond words, but I can't say for sure because I've never seen it."

This surprises Andrew. "Why not?"

"It's in Giverny, about an hour from Paris. You need a car to get there."

For the first time today, thoughts of Julien cross her mind. He had a motorbike. He could have taken her, but every time she asked he had something more important to do.

"Why not rent a car and drive out?" Andrew says.

"I was a student back then with barely enough money to pay the rent. Now..." She scrunches her nose. "It's not much fun going alone."

"No, I meant why don't I rent a car and the two of us can take a ride out there together. I'd like to see it."

"You would? You'd really like to see it?"

"Yes," Andrew answers emphatically. "I really would. Now that you've gotten me into this sightseeing thing, I'm actually enjoying it." He smiles. "Plus having you along makes me feel like I've got my own expert guide."

It is the first time in a number of years, but Max feels her cheeks grow warm. She is blushing. Actually blushing.

"Thanks for the compliment," she says. "But don't you have meetings to go to?"

"I can wrap it up tomorrow morning, then in the afternoon we can do the Louvre and Thursday we can drive out to—Giverny, was it?"

Max nods. "Yes, Giverny."

WHEN THEY FINALLY LEAVE THE museum, it is only because the closing chimes have sounded.

"Time flies in here, doesn't it?" Max says.

Andrew nods. "I never thought I'd enjoy spending time in a museum as much as I have today. Once I got through law school, I wasn't interested in anything that wasn't physical.

My big interests were racquetball, tennis and golf. But today..."

"I've never done even one of those things," Max says, laughing. "So I guess we all find our comfort zone and stay there."

"Well, since you've shown me the joy of a museum, I think it only fair that you let me drag you out for a game of golf. You just might like it."

Max grins. "I'd be terrible. I'm so clumsy I'd embarrass you in front of all your friends, make a fool of myself—"

He chucks her under the chin and tilts her face up toward his. "I doubt you could ever look foolish," he says. There is more to this thought and it is on the tip of his tongue, but it is too soon so he holds the words back.

With his mouth only inches from hers, Max fears he is going to kiss her. She could easily enough be carried away but hopes it will not happen. Although it would be good to feel his mouth pressed against hers he is not Julien, and this friendship is too lovely to spoil with a moment of passion.

She drops her head ever so slightly, but it is enough to take the focus of his eyes from hers.

"Maybe I could do tennis," she says. "It seems a bit less intimidating."

Andrew grins. "Okay, when we get home, it's a date!"

His words cause a worrisome tick in Max's head. She tries to brush it away with the rationale that he is referring to a date not in the romantic sense but simply as a scheduled event to put on the calendar.

She gives him a crooked smile and says, "Okay, we'll schedule a tennis game when we get home."

Now that the thought has become nothing more than a scheduled appointment, Max feels relieved.

"There's a great little café not far from here," she suggests. "Want to grab a bite to eat?"

"Only if you let me pay," Andrew says.

"No way." Max laughs. "You paid yesterday, it's my turn today. Don't forget, I've now got money in my pocket."

"Oh, right." He hooks his arm onto hers and says, "Lead the way."

THE LOUVRE

On Wednesday Andrew arrives at the Lazar Offices before eight; he is anxious to get the meeting started and over with. Thoughts of Max are stuck in his head, and it is impossible to push them aside. Even as John Connor, the Canadian representative, rattles on about the need to revise a clause in the sixth paragraph on the nineteenth page of a contract, he hears Max's voice. Her laughter is warm and her words filled with enthusiasm when she tells the story of one painting or another.

As he thinks back on her delight in Cezanne's *Apples and Oranges*, their first meeting comes to mind. Max had not seen him standing in the doorway as she told Annie, "This better not be a fix-up, because I am not even remotely interested in anything romantic."

Why would she say such a thing, he wonders? There has been no mention of a boyfriend, and yesterday when he leaned in to kiss her she'd held her face to his. Only at the very last moment did she turn away. Why?

Perhaps a bad experience, one such as he'd had with Liza. He'd had plans and the best of intentions. He'd already bought an engagement ring and was simply waiting for the right moment to pop the question. The right moment never came, because she left town with a man she'd known for less than a month. After Liza he didn't date for a full year, and not once has he been inclined to pursue anything more than an occasional concert or a few casual dinners.

"Well, don't you agree?" Connor repeats loudly.

Andrew is caught off guard and stumbles over his words. "Sorry, I was checking the client release form. Can you give me that again?"

Connor reads the entire clause again. It is long and cumbersome, filled with legal terms such as "amicus curiae," "de facto," "concurrent claims" and "ex parte." He speaks in a monotone voice that is as annoying as the hum of a bee.

Andrew feigns interest but is still thinking of Max. When Connor finally finishes speaking, Andrew gives a nod of agreement then says they need to wrap this up as he has another meeting this afternoon.

"I've several more contract issues to review," Connor says.

Andrew knows these are nit-picky things. A word here, a word there, endless hours of listening to a man who simply wants to command center stage for as long as possible. He glances down at his watch. It is already eleven.

"I have to leave," he says, "but why don't you continue the meeting and send me the minutes with any agreed upon changes."

"What if you don't agree with the changes?" Connor asks.

"Don't worry, I'll agree."

"Without hearing them through?"

"I trust your judgment," Andrew says. He opens his briefcase, places his copies of the contract and agenda on top, shakes hands with Peter Lazar and leaves.

MAX IS LEAFING THROUGH A magazine in the lobby of the Hotel Baltimore when he hurries in.

"You're early," she says.

Andrew smiles. "The meeting wrapped up earlier than expected. I thought maybe we could have lunch before going to the Louvre."

"You like sandwiches?" she asks.

When he answers yes, she suggests they buy baguettes and eat outside. "We can sit by the fountain in front of the Louvre. It's a beautiful day."

"Yes, beautiful." When Andrew says this he is again looking at Max's face. She is even lovelier than he'd remembered. As she stands and hooks her arm through his, a stray thought in the back of his head warns, *Be careful.* He ignores it.

"Sandwiches it is," he says, and off they go.

After they have picked up ham and cheese baguettes he stops at the wine shop, buys a bottle of Chateau Saint-Maur Rose and asks for plastic cups. The shopkeeper gives him a look of chagrin and reluctantly hands him the cups.

"This fine wine deserves a crystal glass," he says sourly.

Andrew laughs. "Perhaps. But today I am picnicking with a mademoiselle who deserves fine wine."

The shopkeeper gives an understanding nod.

Max overhears what Andrew says to the shopkeeper, and the words warm her heart. She is no longer a stupid woman robbed by the man she once loved; she is now a woman deserving of fine wine.

WHEN THEY REACH THE LOUVRE, they settle on the ledge alongside the pool in front of the pyramid. The fountains are on, and ripples gently float across the surface of the water. He opens the wine, fills a plastic cup and hands it to Max. He then fills his own cup and raises it.

"A toast to milady," he says laughingly.

She raises her own cup. "And to my charming escort."

Max means what she says. Andrew is charming. And handsome. Not in the perfect way of Julien, but softer, more casual.

Most times Max is anxious to hurry inside. Even if she were to have years, there would never be enough time for seeing all there is to see at the Louvre. But today she is in no hurry. They linger over lunch for nearly an hour, talking about anything and everything. He tells her of his years at law school, and she tells him of her previous visit to Paris. Still there is no mention of Julien.

When she asks if he has ever been serious with anyone, he nods.

"Liza Berkowitz," he says. "I was going to ask her to marry me, but..." The remainder he leaves unsaid. For both of them the stigma of being jilted is like a basket of dirty laundry, something to be shoved to the back of the closet and not aired.

AFTER LUNCH THEY ENTER THE museum, satisfyingly full and just a bit giddy. The wine was light and slightly fruity, the kind that goes down easily and leaves a mellow afterglow.

Max asks if Andrew would like earphones for a guided tour, but he shakes his head.

"I like to listen to you explain everything." There is a pause; then he looks down at her with a broad smile and adds, "You see things other people don't see."

What Andrew doesn't say is that he is enchanted by everything about her, by the sparkle in her eyes, by the way she sees beauty in the curve of an arm or the arch of a doorway. He likes simply hearing the sound of her voice and would be just as willing to listen if she were reading a list of names from the telephone book.

Max gives him a soft smile. She takes a measure of pride in the fact that he wants her to explain the works of art.

They spend the afternoon going from floor to floor, joining the throng standing wide-eyed in front of the Mona Lisa and then moving on to the sculpture hall. Max stops in front of the marble Winged Victory.

"They say this was sculpted two hundred years before Christ was born," she whispers.

"Why is she headless?" Andrew whispers back.

Max shrugs. "When they unearthed the statue, they never found the head. They found parts of the hand, but never the head." She gives a sigh as if this is a troubling thing.

When they turn to leave there is a crowd behind them. Andrew wraps his arm around her waist and guides her through a group of Japanese tourists.

Max is a bit surprised by how much she enjoys the feel of his hand on her waist, and she makes no move to shrug it off. As they move beyond the crowd, she turns her face to his.

"Thank you," she says.

He stops and turns her to face him. "For what?" he asks and pulls her a bit closer. Again his mouth is inches from hers.

"For saving me from a ruined vacation," she says.

"It's my pleasure," he says and lowers his face to hers. A thought in the back of his mind screams, *Too soon, too soon!* but he ignores it and lifts his hand from her waist to the arch in the back of her neck.

Andrew is only a breath away from kissing her when a tourist backs into him and sends him stumbling forward. His forehead slams against hers and she yells, "Ouch!"

The tourist holds his hand up. "So sorry, so sorry."

"No problem," Andrew says, faking a laugh. He doesn't feel like laughing, but at the moment it's all he can do.

MAX IS STILL THINKING OF that moment when they leave the museum. She is equally disappointed and glad the kiss didn't happen. The last thing in the world she wants is mixed emotions over another guy.

She tells herself that with Andrew it is a friendship. A very good friendship; one she wants to hold on to and keep exactly as it is. Simple. Uncomplicated.

A small voice in the back of her mind whispers, *Really?*

MAX

I f Monday you've have told me that two days later I'd have the most wonderful evening imaginable, I would have laughed in your face. But that's exactly what happened. All along I thought I was showing Andrew around Paris, but tonight he took me to a place I've heard of a thousand times but never once set foot in. The Bleu Train. It's in the old Gare de Leon train station, but the way it's decorated you'd think you were dining at Versailles.

When I asked how he knew about this place, he kind of blushed. "The concierge at the hotel," he said. He is so blasted cute when he blushes like that. One minute he's like this powerful lion who will take care of you and solve all your problems; then the next minute he's blushing like a shy little boy. He was still blushing when he told me that he had an open-ended business class ticket home and changed it from Thursday to Sunday so that we'd fly back the same day. Isn't that sweet?

I hadn't intended to tell him about Julien, but I did. I don't know whether it was because of the wine or just the fact that he's so easy to talk to. I feel like I could tell Andrew almost anything and he'd never be judgmental. He did, however, look sort of sad when I told him I'd come to Paris looking for Julien.

"Too bad," he said, then moved on to asking what I'd like for dessert.

The one thing I didn't tell him was that Julien was part of the group who robbed me. That's too shameful to even admit.

I have to say, there are moments when I feel kind of attracted to Andrew. He's not at all what I'd consider my type, but sometimes when he leans close to me and I get a whiff of his aftershave or feel his skin brush against mine I get this tingly sensation in the pit of my stomach.

Crazy, right?

Andrew is cute and he's a great guy, but the truth is I'm still in love with Julien. I know he's a horrible person, a person who lies, steals and God knows what else. I have every reason in the world to hate him with all my heart, but I don't. I want to; I swear I do, but I keep remembering the way he could send chills up and down my spine with nothing more than a touch of his hand.

Julien is a sickness inside of me. All I can do right now is hope and pray that in time I'll be able to rid myself of him. Then maybe my heart will heal, and I'll be able to love somebody else.

AFTER THE STORM

All day Tuesday and again Wednesday Annie, Oliver and even Ophelia work at cleaning debris from the house and yard. Oliver saws the tree trunk into stump-sized pieces and one by one carries them to the far edge of the property where they will eventually be hauled away. Although Annie's stomach is round and cumbersome, she still bends to pick up the small branches and pieces of shingle ripped from the roof. Ophelia has mopped three buckets of water from the kitchen, and still there is more.

The storm has left nothing untouched. The storage shed has a broken window. Several trees are missing branches. The huge willow leans like a weary woman, and the early plantings in the garden are gone. In some spots there is a lone plant that has survived, but even those are few and far between.

The wisteria bushes alongside the house are flattened to the ground. Oliver takes some of the boards from the porch and chops one end into a point. He uses these boards as stakes and drives them into the ground. He is hopeful that tied to a stake the wisteria will survive.

A number of times he tries to call Judge Rogers, but even on the landlines the service is spotty at best. When he finally does get through he learns that a string of tornados cut a swath straight through Wyattsville, Dorchester and Burnsville.

"So far there have been seven deaths," Rogers says. "Good thing you left early Monday evening; anyone who was on Carlson Road at that time..."

There is no need for Rogers to finish the sentence; they both know the ending.

Oliver gives a silent sigh of relief. This is the route he takes home every evening, and most evenings he is an hour or two later coming home. On Monday Annie asked him to leave early. She said Ophelia wanted to come and stay the night.

Odd, he thinks. Not since the day Ophelia left Memory House has she come back to spend the night, and yet on this night...

"No," he mumbles and shakes his head. It's not possible...is it?

It is a strange thing to be smack in the middle of a disaster and yet know so little of it, but that's precisely how it is. There is news coming out of Richmond, which is well beyond the storm track, but Oliver only catches bits and pieces of it on the decades-old portable radio they found in the basement. Gathering the batteries from three clocks and a flashlight, the best he can do is get a scratchy-voiced signal that comes and goes.

On Wednesday morning a note is posted to the courthouse door saying that all proceedings are cancelled for the remainder of the week. Most of the stores in downtown Wyattsville remain closed. The electricity is still out, and without power credit card terminals and cash registers are inoperable. Before the day is gone the meat in the freezer and refrigerated cases of the Mighty Mart starts to have an odd smell and has to be thrown out. It cannot even be given away because the threat of salmonella is too great.

By Wednesday evening Annie has checked her cell phone

twenty-six times and has gotten the same message every time: Service not available.

"How is this possible?" she asks.

Oliver is busy sanding the scratches the tree limb left in the dining room table. He stops for a moment and looks up.

"The cell tower is probably down," he says, then goes back to sanding. "We may have to send this out and have it refinished. These scratches are too deep."

"So we'll have it refinished," Annie says impatiently. "Now about the cell phone, is there any way—"

"Use the landline." He frowns at the spot he's just sanded. "We're definitely going to have to send it out."

"I don't want to make a call," Annie says. "I'm waiting for a message from Max. I haven't heard from her since last Thursday."

"Don't worry, I'm sure everything is fine."

"It isn't fine if she isn't answering my messages."

"Don't worry," he repeats. "We should have power by tomorrow."

"If the power comes back, will we have cell service?"

Oliver shrugs. "It's hard to say."

AFTER A SECOND DAY OF hard work and a candlelight supper, everyone is ready for bed.

"Let's call it a day," Oliver says.

Ophelia agrees.

Annie wrinkles her nose. "I'm still worried about Max. I wanted to check my messages before we go to bed."

Ophelia again tells her there is nothing to worry about.

"Max is fine," she says. "I can feel it in my bones."

Annie sighs. "Even so, I'd be happier if she answered my text."

"Bring the phone upstairs with you," Oliver says through a yawn. "You can check it later."

Annie carries the phone upstairs and places it on the nightstand beside the bed. Moments before she closes her eyes she checks the screen. Still no service.

Long after Oliver is sound asleep, she is tossing and turning. It is so unlike Max to ignore a text. Something has to be wrong.

AT 3:40AM THURSDAY MORNING A text message beeps. Annie is only half asleep so she reaches out and grabs the phone. It blinks *1 New Message.*

She clicks on the message.

"Your service has now been restored," it reads. "We apologize for any inconvenience this disruption has caused."

There is no message from Max.

Now Annie is truly worried. She lights the small candle and carries it out to the landing. She sits on the top step and taps out another message, this time in an email. If this goes unanswered, she is uncertain what she will do.

> Max – We had a terrible storm and our power has been out since Monday night. Have you tried to send a message? I am really worried about you. Did you find Julien? Please don't be sad if you haven't. I know you believe you still love him, but 3 years is a long time and if you give your heart a chance you will find a new love. Are you still at the Hotel Vendome? Is everything OK? Text me and let me know. If I don't hear from you by tomorrow, I am going to track you down.
> Love, Annie

In the subject line she types IMPORTANT; then she clicks Send.

GOING TO GIVERNY

On Thursday morning Andrew is at the Vendome before ten o'clock. A white convertible is parked alongside the curb, and in his pocket is a list of places to visit while they are in Giverny. He hopes this day will go as planned. Already it is looking good; the sky is clear and bright, and it is warm for this time of year.

Max steps out of the elevator just as he enters the lobby.

"Perfect timing," he says then crosses over and kisses her cheek. It is the type of kiss friends often share; a greeting, nothing more. He would like it to be more, but now and again she still speaks of the boyfriend she came in search of.

Over the past few days Andrew feels himself drawing closer to Max, and while he is wary this might be a mistake he can do nothing to stop it. She is unlike any woman he has ever known. There is magic in the ease of her laugh and a fierce intensity in her love of art. When she speaks her words have a simple earnestness; there is no pretense.

She is a woman he could easily fall in love with, but it is too soon. Much too soon. For now he will content himself with simply being her friend.

Keeping it casual, he loops his arm through hers and they head for the front door. As they pass the front desk, the clerk gives a nod and a friendly "Bonjour."

ANDREW OPENS THE CAR DOOR and waits for Max to sit.

"I hope you don't mind a convertible," he says. "I thought once we were out in the country—"

"Are you kidding, I love it!" Max looks up and smiles. "If you'd have asked, this is exactly what I would have chosen."

He circles around the back of the car, climbs behind the wheel and pulls away from the curb. It is bumper-to-bumper traffic as they wend their way through the streets of Paris, but once they pass La Defense he turns onto a highway. There is still a steady stream of cars, but they move along.

Paris is a city that has grown beyond its borders. On the outskirts they pass neighborhoods lined with apartment buildings that are strangely similar to those in the city, except many of these terraces are crowded with baby toys and an occasional rack of laundry set out to dry. After several miles the buildings become smaller and eventually are replaced by single-family houses bunched together like tiny towns. Between the towns are long stretches of grasslands and farms.

"I've never been out this way before," Max says.

"I'm glad," Andrew replies. "It's nice to have a new experience that belongs only to us." While his words still hang in the air, he thinks this is something he should have left unsaid. It has the sound of a couple moving into a relationship. He is about to swing into an apology when Max turns with a smile lighting her face.

"You're right," she says. "Thinking of it that way makes this trip seem even more special." She reaches across and gives his arm an affectionate squeeze.

For a few moments her eyes linger on his face. He is looking to the road ahead, but his lips have the hint of a smile. The wind has ruffled his hair, and a curl has fallen onto his forehead. She is tempted to brush it back, but the truth is she likes the look of it.

For a fleeting second she pictures Julien: dark eyes and slicked back hair, a long stride that sometimes left her lagging behind. She gives a deep sigh; it is partly regret and partly relief. Although she cannot say she no longer loves Julien, Andrew is a pleasant change. He has a boyish charm and an easy-going manner that makes him fun to be with.

GIVERNY IS A CENTURIES-OLD stone village. The town has risen up around the artist it celebrates, so there is only one main road and it is named Rue Claude Monet. Andrew follows signs pointing the way to the house and garden. When they finally arrive there is not a single parking space left, and the line in front of the house runs the full length of the block. Andrew maneuvers a tight three-point turn, and they head back down the road lined with gardens, historical sites and restaurants.

"There's got to be a parking spot somewhere along here," he says. At the far end of the road he doubles back and turns down Rue du Milieu, a small cobblestone side road. At Le Maison d'hote, he pulls into one of few remaining parking spaces.

"Want to brave the line or do lunch first?" he asks.

"Brave the line," Max answers. As they start toward the road, she glances back over her shoulder at the stone house with its large porch and a patio filled with umbrella tables.

"This looks like a cute place," she says. "After we tour the house and gardens, let's have dinner here."

Andrew's mouth stretches into a wide smile. "Sounds good to me."

It is a long walk back to the Monet house, and the line is

almost as long as it was earlier. By the time they enter it is nearing two o'clock.

Passing by a tiny blue sitting room, they move through the remainder of the house. Max stops to study everything: the Japanese prints hanging on the walls, the family photographs, a small planter, a worn dresser. Andrew watches her. He has no need to see these things for himself; he is seeing them through her eyes, and he is certain they are more beautiful that way.

In the studio a large window bathes the room in sunlight. When she closes her eyes she can see Monet standing at the easel and can breathe in the smell of turpentine and oils. She leans over to Andrew and whispers, "Can't you just feel him still in this room?"

He smiles at the wide-eyed expression on her face. "I definitely feel something," he whispers back.

She remains in the studio for almost forty minutes. Other tourists come and go, but Max and Andrew stay. Max studies the smallest detail in each painting and revels in the aura that comes from within the walls. She wants to capture every nuance of the room so that years from now, perhaps when she is as old as Ophelia, she will be able to call this memory to mind and feel what she has tucked away.

In time they move through to the huge kitchen with its white tiles and copper pots hanging along the wall. From there they step out into the traditional English garden. It is ablaze with narcissi, tulips, daffodils and pansies. Although it is early in the season, even the cherry and crab apple trees are in full bloom.

Andrew pulls out his cell phone. "Stay there," he tells Max. "I want to take your picture." He clicks off four shots then shows her the pictures.

"Ooh, look at those colors," she squeals. "Let's do one together." Before he can answer she grabs the arm of a passing tourist and asks if he will take their picture.

He nods and accepts the phone that is offered. "Smile," he says. He touches his finger to the button and holds it there a bit too long so there is a burst of 11 shots. In every one of the pictures, Max is grinning at the camera and Andrew is smiling down at her.

Max scrolls through the pictures. "These are awesome. Would you send them to me?"

"Of course," Andrew says. "What's your email?"

She rumbles through the spelling of Architect-Max-at g-mail then adds, "While you're at it maybe you should program in my home number. You might need it."

"Good idea," he says happily.

After strolling through the lanes of flowering plants, they wander over to the Japanese water garden and the mood changes.

"Here is where he painted the water lilies," Max says. The sky has become overcast, and the giant weeping willows start to fade into the darkening clouds. Andrew turns on the flash and takes two more pictures of Max. In one she is standing alongside the painted railing of a small bridge. The other is a close-up profile shot with her looking down into the pond.

When the second flash goes off she is momentarily startled.

"Oh, darn, I wasn't looking at the camera," she says.

"I know." Andrew clicks on the photo icon and smiles at the picture he has taken. This is the one he likes best.

Max then insists they take a selfie. They stand with their heads close to one another, her cheek pressed tight against his. With the phone in his hand, he stretches his arm out and snaps the picture.

"Let's see what it looks like," she says, and he scrolls over to photos.

The picture is so close it seems distorted. They are both wearing goofy-looking grins. Max laughs like this is the funniest thing she's ever seen. Her laugh is contagious, and seconds later Andrew is caught up in it. They take two more selfies, and each is funnier than the one before.

The six o'clock chimes have already rung when they make their way out of the garden. The gray clouds are lower now, and the smell of rain is in the air.

Andrew stops at the gift shop and raps on the glass panel. The door is locked, but the attendant is still inside. She looks up and sees him motioning to the display of floral umbrellas. She points to her watch and shakes her head no. Andrew puts his hands together as if in prayer. Then holds up a ten-euro note and mouths the words *For you*. Again he gives her a pleading look.

She laughs, pulls an umbrella from the display and carries it to the door. She opens only the top section of the door and passes the umbrella out.

"Twenty-five euros plus tax," she says. He hands her forty euros and tells her to keep the change.

THEY ARE ONLY HALFWAY DOWN Rue du Milieu when the sky opens up and fat raindrops begin falling. Andrew pushes the umbrella up and curls his arm around Max.

"Stay close," he says, "so you don't get wet."

The Telephone Call

When Annie wakes on Thursday morning the first thing she does is check her cell phone. No new messages.

Before Oliver's eyes are open she says, "Our cell phone service came back on at three-thirty this morning, and there was no message from Max."

He sits up, rubs his eyes then glances at the clock.

"It's a quarter till seven," he says wearily. "Go back to sleep."

"I can't sleep; I'm too worried."

"Don't worry," he says, stifling a yawn. "She's probably just busy."

"No, you don't understand. When the power came on I sent her an email and said it was important that she get back to me right away."

"At three o'clock in the morning?"

"It was three-forty and anyway in Paris it was nine-forty. Now it's almost one o'clock there."

Oliver turns to her with one eye partly closed. "Maybe she doesn't want to disturb people while they're sleeping," he says and plops back down on the pillow.

"I'm not sleeping. And besides—"

Oliver half opens one eye. "I'm sleeping."

"No, you're not," Annie argues. "What if something has happened to Max? What if she's in trouble? Or needs help?"

Oliver lifts himself onto one elbow. "Nothing has happened to Max. She's a smart girl; if she's in trouble or needs something, she'll call. So just relax and let me get another half-hour of sleep, okay?" He drops back and turns on his side.

"What if she can't call?" Annie grumbles. "Then what?"

Before her feet hit the floor she has decided. If she doesn't hear from Max by twelve noon, she is calling the Hotel Vendome. By then it will be 6PM in Paris. Max will have had a whole day to answer. A day is long enough to wait for a response. If there is no response by then, Annie will know something is wrong.

ONCE THE POWER IS BACK on it would seem that life can return to normal, but Burnsville is like a sleeping bear and it is slow to awaken. Now that the danger is past, Ophelia is ready to return home. She mentions this at breakfast, and Oliver volunteers to drive her.

"Are you sure you don't want to stay a few more days?" Annie asks. With Max gone and unaccounted for, she hopes Ophelia will say yes but she doesn't.

"I've got to get back," she says. "Lillian's birthday is Saturday and—"

"But today's only Thursday," Annie says. "And I was hoping you'd stay with me because I'm worried about Max."

Ophelia gives a big hearty laugh. "I told you, there's no need to worry about Max. She's just fine."

"How can you possibly know that? I've texted her three times—I've even emailed her!—and she hasn't once answered me!"

"Pshaw," Ophelia chuffs. "Sending messages back and forth

across an ocean can't tell you the truth of how a person is doing. That's something you've got to feel in your bones."

"Well, then, how come I don't feel it?"

"Because you're too busy worrying."

None of this makes any sense to Annie, and an hour later when she kisses Ophelia goodbye her face is still twisted into a worrisome frown. As she watches Oliver's car pull out of the driveway, she hears the grandfather clock chiming. She counts the gongs: ten. Two hours until noon. Annie is uncertain whether she can wait that long.

THERE IS PLENTY TO DO now that the power is back on, so Annie tries to busy herself. Hopefully this will make the time go faster. She gathers the towels used to wipe the storm water from the floor, stuffs them in the washer and adds a cup of detergent. Although she has already cleaned the kitchen she goes over it again, swishing a rag across the counters and appliances. She even wipes the dust from the repotted philodendron sitting on the kitchen windowsill, but none of these things stop her from thinking about Max.

She eyes the clock hanging above the kitchen door: 11:02. Impossible, she thinks. Surely it has been more than an hour since Oliver left with Ophelia. She pulls the small stepladder from the closet, climbs up and lifts the clock from its hook. Holding it to her ear she listens. The battery is still buzzing and the second hand tick-tick-ticking. She places the clock back on its hook and steps down.

She stands there for a moment then pulls the cell phone from her pocket and checks. Still no new message. Not even an advertisement or a spam email saying she's won a million dollars.

What's the sense in waiting, Annie asks herself. In Paris it's already after five, more than enough time for Max to have answered. What's the difference in an hour more or less? She goes to the desk and pulls out the paper Max has left with her.

She dials 011 then 33 for France, then the area code and telephone number for the Hotel Vendome. There is a slight delay, but to Annie it seems way too long. Finally the phone connects, and a man answers on the third ring.

"Bonjour," he says. "Hotel Vendome."

"Do you have a Max Martinelli staying there?" Annie asks.

"You mean Maxine Martinelli?"

Of course, Max has used the name on her passport. "Yes, Maxine," Annie answers. "May I speak with her please?"

"Mademoiselle Martinelli is out just now."

"I'm her best friend," Annie explains, "and I haven't heard from her, so I've been terribly worried. Have you seen her today? Is she okay? She's not hurt or—"

He chuckles. "I would say Mademoiselle Martinelli is very okay. She left here in her young man's automobile this morning. I imagine they are off for a day of fun."

Annie releases a sigh of relief. "Thank goodness. I was so worried."

Again the clerk reassures her there is nothing to be concerned about.

Not wanting to act like a mother hen hovering over Max while she is off having fun, Annie tells the clerk he needn't bother leaving a message.

THAT AFTERNOON ANNIE CALLS OPHELIA.

"You were right," she says. "I was foolish to worry. Max is with Julien, and they are off having fun."

Since this is such a change of attitude, Ophelia asks if Annie has gotten a message or spoken to Max.

"No," Annie replies, "but I can feel it in my bones."

Ophelia gives another jolly laugh.

A LATE DATE

By the time Andrew and Max reach Le Maison d'hote, the air has grown cold and they are chilled to the bone. The inn with its crackling fire and glowing chandeliers is more than inviting. As they settle into the plush round chairs, Andrew suggests they start with an aperitif wine and appetizers.

"I don't know about you," he says, "but I'm famished."

Max laughs. "I'm beyond famished. I've already moved on to starving."

Whether it is the warmth of the fire or the mellowness of the Dubonnet neither of them can say, but the world outside is all but forgotten. It is only the two of them, leaning into each other's words, sharing stories and reliving moments of the past few days.

"It seems hard to believe that at first we didn't like each other," Max says.

"You didn't like me," Andrew corrects her, "but I thought you were adorable. Then you hit me with 'I'm not interested in anything the least bit romantic'." He mimics her in a squeaky female voice.

"You do terrible imitations," she says laughingly. "I don't sound one bit like that!"

169

"Yeah, I guess you don't," he chuckles.

"Anyway, I was within my rights. After all you did call me a loser."

Andrew gives an over-exaggerated gasp. "I never!"

"You most certainly did. When I told you Brianna said I was a loser because I didn't have a real office, you agreed."

Andrew leans forward and cups her chin in the palm of his hand. "No, I agreed you should have an office, but you didn't give me a chance to finish what I wanted to say. You jumped up from the table in a huff, and that was the end of that."

"You had something else to say?"

He nods. "I was going to tell you I have an empty office that you're welcome to use for as long as you like."

"You're kidding."

"No, I'm not. It's Oliver's old office, but from the look of things he's not coming back to the practice." Andrew tilts his head, gives a sexy smile and keeps his eyes locked on Max's. "It's yours if you want it."

Max leans across the corner of the table to kiss Andrew. She means to kiss his cheek, but he turns and their lips meet. It is intended as a simple thank you kiss, but something happens. They both feel it.

When she pulls back, Max is blushing.

"I'm sorry," she stammers. "I didn't mean to—"

"Don't apologize," Andrew says. "I've been wanting to do that all day."

THE APERITIFS AND APPETIZERS GIVE way to a bottle of burgundy and dinner. He samples the morsels of duck she holds to his mouth.

"Now you've got to try my fillet," he says. He cuts off a sliver and lifts it to her lips. After the steak he feeds her a mushroom that he claims is as sweet as champagne. As she takes the mushroom into her mouth he sees the joy of this day glistening in her eyes and says, "You look very beautiful tonight."

"With my mouth full of mushroom?" She laughs.

"Yes," he answers. "Even with your mouth full of mushroom."

OUTSIDE THE RAIN CONTINUES. IT rolls off the tiles of the roof and puddles in the pathway. The road grows muddy and the cobblestones slick, but right now this is of no concern. They hear only the crackle of the fire and the soft strains of a violin player who strolls from room to room.

After dinner there is brandy and petit fours. It would seem that in time they would run out of things to say, but this doesn't happen. Instead one word leads to another; a single story grows into a tale and secrets are whispered back and forth.

It is nearing eleven when from the corner of his eye Andrew sees the restaurant owner pacing back and forth. The violinist is gone, and the dining room adjacent to theirs is already darkened. He pulls his eyes from Max, glances around the room then whispers, "We're the only people left in this restaurant."

She giggles and looks around. "Oh my gosh, we are."

Andrew signals for the check.

"I think I'll run to the ladies room before we leave." Max stands then quickly reaches out and grabs for the back of the chair.

"Wow," she says, "I'm really feeling that last brandy!"

The sound of rain is louder now; they hear the splash of it cascading off the roof. Until this moment there has been only the warmth of the room, but now she pictures the dark winding roads covered with a slick of rain and mud. She pinches her brows together and gives Andrew a look of apprehension.

"Are you alright to drive?" she asks.

"I think so," he says hesitantly, "but..." He leaves that thought hanging and asks, "Would you prefer we get rooms here and wait until morning to start back?"

When Max answers her words are pushed together, jittery and nervous sounding.

"Sleep here?" she says. "I don't think so. It's too soon, it's—"

"Whoa," Andrew cuts in. "That's not what I'm suggesting. With all this rain and as much as we've had to drink, I just thought it might be safer if we—"

"Oh." Max gives a sigh of relief.

When the owner returns with the receipt, Andrew asks if the inn can give them two rooms for the night.

"Non," he says and shakes his head sorrowfully, "But I have one chambre with two beds."

Max's eyes light up. She looks at Andrew and nods.

"Perfect," he says.

AFTER ANDREW SIGNS THE REGISTER, the innkeeper hands him the key and says the room is left at the top of the stairs. "Number nine," he adds.

Max expects a small room with narrow twin beds, but this room has a cozy sitting area, a fireplace waiting to be lit and two wide double beds. Once they are inside with the door closed behind them, there is an awkward silence.

"Maybe this wasn't such a good idea," Max says nervously.

Andrew raises his hands palms out. "You don't have to worry about me. I would never—"

"Sully my reputation?" she laughs.

He chuckles. "I was going to say try something, but sully your reputation works just as well."

As they chat Max walks around the room tracing her finger

around the lace doily on the dresser and fidgeting with the tasseled key in the Victorian wardrobe. When the wardrobe door pops open she peers inside. There are two fleecy white robes hanging on the hooks. Above them there is a sign that reads, "Pour l' utilisation de nos invitees" — *For the use of our guests.*

"Cool," she says, pulling out one of the robes. "We can use these to sleep in." She takes the robe and disappears into the bathroom. Soon there is the sound of the shower, and fifteen minutes later Max reappears. She is wrapped in the robe with her face scrubbed shiny clean and her hair damp from the shower.

"That felt great," she says. "You ought to try it."

"Think I will," Andrew says. He removes his shirt, tosses it on the back of the chair and grabs the other robe.

As he disappears into the bathroom, Max looks at his back. He is slightly tanned and well muscled. Not quite as tall as Julien but almost as well built. It's something she hadn't noticed until now. She also hadn't noticed the way the back of his hair curls at his neck. *Nice,* she thinks.

WHEN ANDREW RETURNS HE ALSO is wrapped in a robe.

"You're right," he says. "This shower is great."

Max is sitting in one of the beds. "The only problem with the shower is that now I'm not the least bit sleepy."

Andrew plops down on the other bed. "Neither am I."

Within a span of minutes they are once again involved in a conversation. It seems somehow odd that people who four months earlier barely spoke to one another now have so much to say. The conversation moves easily from one topic to the next. Andrew talks about his years of law school, and she tells how she came to be an architect.

"It started when I was nine," she says. "On my way to school I used to pass by an old house that was boarded up and left to rot.

You could tell that in its day the house had been beautiful, and I couldn't help but wonder why the owner didn't fix it up. Then one morning I passed by and saw a crew of workmen. I was so happy. I thought for sure the owner was finally going to fix up that lovely house, but, no, they were there to take it down." Max shakes her head and gives a saddened sigh. "When they ripped the porch loose from that house, I actually heard it scream."

"I can believe that," Andrew says.

"I'm glad you can, because my daddy didn't. That night I told him how I'd heard the house scream, and he said such talk was pure nonsense."

Andrew frowns. "Not very sensitive, was he?"

"Not at all. But he made me realize there are a lot of people just like him. They think a building is nothing but a pile of wood and bricks. That's because they don't take the time to stop and listen for what the building has to say. Buildings actually have a soul the same as people."

The small bachelor's chest between the two beds has a lamp with a flared shade atop it. To look Andrew in the eye Max has to lean forward and peer around the lamp. After a short while, she says, "I'm getting a kink in my neck; you mind if I move over there beside you?"

He grins and says, "It would be my pleasure."

She moves over, sits beside him and leans her head on his shoulder. "Ah, much better," she murmurs.

"Yeah." He slides his arm around her shoulder and repeats, "Much better."

They talk until the wee hours of the morning, and when they finally fall asleep she is still in his arms.

IT IS ALMOST EIGHT O'CLOCK when a ray of sunlight shines

through the leaded glass window and wakes Max. The moment she stirs, Andrew wakes.

She looks up at him and smiles. "I guess I fell asleep in your bed."

"It would appear so," he says with a smile.

MAX

Waking up next to Andrew was a strange experience, to say the least. I don't know if I'm relieved that nothing happened or I'm wishing it had. I liked the feel of his arms around me. He's gentle and sweet, plus he's really handsome. I didn't notice it at first, but the more time I spend with him the more obvious it becomes.

The thing is I really like Andrew. A lot. It would be very easy to let myself fall in love with him, but I hold back because he deserves something better. He deserves a woman who will give him her whole heart. A woman who can love him as much as he should be loved. Right now I can't do that. A part of me still belongs to Julien.

I know how foolish such a feeling is and I've tried to force myself to let it go, but it's impossible. I remember how it was with us and I keep asking myself, what went wrong? Did I do something? Say something? What? I just can't understand how he could be so in love with me and then just walk away with not a word of explanation.

I hate him for doing that. Truly hate him. I'd like to think that if he showed up on my doorstep begging me to take him back I'd be strong enough to slam the door in his face. The truth is I don't know what I'd do.

Julien has a way about him that draws you in. You know how dangerous he is, and yet you let yourself believe he is sincere. You believe it, because it's what you want to believe. A man like Julien takes everything and gives you nothing. A man like Andrew takes nothing and gives you everything; that's why I could never do anything to hurt him.

Perhaps once I get home and am away from all the things that remind me of Julien, I'll be able to forget him. I pray that in time his face will become a grainy picture too blurry to see and his words will no longer echo in my ear.

When that happens I don't doubt I can fall in love with Andrew — if he hasn't given up on me by then.

Nothing in this life is guaranteed. Nothing. The things you love are like the puffs of a dandelion weed; they grow wild and happen as they will. You pluck a dandelion puff from the ground and hold on to it thinking you own it, but when the wind blows it's gone and all you can do is stand there looking at the emptiness of your hand.

A LIFE OF LIES

Julien is unable to forget Max. Her face is there whenever he closes his eyes. He hears her speak his name and reach out with a look that is astonished and yet loving. He remembers how it used to be and senses that she also remembers. The proof of it was in her eyes. In the way his name rolled off her tongue.

He wonders how he could have been so foolish as to say only *I'm sorry*. A pitiful offering that told nothing of his feelings. He should have spoken the truth: that he'd thought of her a thousand times, perhaps ten thousand times, that no woman has ever really replaced her.

When he pictures Max sitting in the café waiting for him to come, the bitter taste of bile rises into his throat and regret pulses through his body. He could have been more clever and found an excuse for slipping away. He should have met her at the café regardless of the cost.

This thought picks at Julien. It is there day and night. He is torn between what he wants and what he needs. Brigitte, with her quick hands and eagerness to please, is his bread and butter. With her he has no worries. There is no need to venture out in the rain and cold to sell sketches. There is no expectation of greatness.

True, she has a temper that flares like dry timber and is quick to see through deception, but in time she will let down her guard and it will be as it always is. They will make love, he will whisper the words she wants to hear and she will believe them. She believes because it is what she wants to believe.

For four days Julien says nothing more about Max's phone. Twice he takes Brigitte to the café for dinner, and three times they make love. On Thursday morning he hears her stirring but feigns sleep. He is hoping she will do as she often does: pull on a pair of jeans and trot to the boulangerie for fresh croissants.

She sits up, stretches, then swings her feet to the floor and stands. He knows these sounds, so he waits. He has been patient for four days; he can continue to be patient a bit longer.

The splash of water comes from the bathroom; she is rinsing her face and brushing her teeth. She pads softly back to the bedroom, pulls her jeans from the back of the chair and slides into them. Circling the bed, she peers down at Julien. He seems to be sleeping, so she tiptoes from the room and closes the door behind her.

He remains still and listens. Even after he hears the click of the apartment door closing, he waits. She is tricky, and it is not beyond her to slip back into the room to check on him. He ticks off the seconds until a full two minutes have passed, then climbs from the bed and checks the street below. She is halfway down Rue du Garrett and headed for the boulangerie. He glances over at the clock: 9:40AM. He has five, maybe ten minutes.

Dragging the suitcase from beneath the bed, Julien begins his search. Several of the phones have already gone dead; those he sets aside. He is powering on the fourth phone when he hears a faint beep-beep signaling a text message. It is a muffled sound, close by but not from the phones in the suitcase. He yanks the nightstand drawer open and rummages through Brigitte's collection of lacy panties and brassieres. Nothing.

The beep-beep sounds a second time. It is closer than before. Julien slides his arm between the mattress and box spring and searches. He feels the vibration before his fingers touch the phone.

She knew I would search, he thinks as he pulls the phone from its hiding place. When he spies the pink case, he is certain this is the phone he has been looking for. He pushes the button and the screen lights. A message indicates there is only two percent battery remaining. He slides his finger across the unlock bar and a number keyboard appears on the screen. Max has the phone locked. A password code is needed to unlock it.

Damn, he grumbles.

He tries to remember her birthday. September...September 16th. He enters 0916.

"Incorrect password," the screen flashes.

Perhaps it was the eighteenth. He enters 0918. Again he gets "Incorrect password."

The apartment door clicks open, so he slams the suitcase shut and shoves it back under the bed. He grabs his jeans from the floor, stuffs the phone into the pocket then drops them back into the same spot.

When Brigitte opens the door, he is sitting on the side of the bed. He gives a lazy smile then stretches his arms and yawns.

"Where were you?" he asks.

"At the boulangerie," she says. "I bought fresh croissants for breakfast." She crosses the room, wraps her arms around his neck and lowers her face to his.

"Did you miss me?" she teases.

"Of course," he answers.

She covers his mouth with hers in a soft kiss. "Come, let's have breakfast. We can plan what to do today."

Julien smiles then playfully smacks her on the behind. "Go make coffee. I'll be there in a few moments."

He tries to pretend everything is as it always is, but

unfortunately it is not. Now that he has Max's phone, she is again at the forefront of his mind.

As Julien pulls on his jeans, he considers what needs to be done. First he must recharge the phone; then, given time, he will be able to figure out the password. It is four digits. A date or perhaps part of a telephone number or a building address.

Brigitte has a charging cord in the kitchen drawer. When she turns her back he will grab it and disappear into the bathroom. With the door closed he will have privacy and time to experiment with the code.

BY THE TIME JULIEN COMES into the kitchen, Brigitte has poured the coffee and set the basket of croissants on the table.

"Butter or jam?" she asks.

"Um, butter," he says absently. "My stomach is feeling a bit off."

"Poor baby." She puts her hand to his forehead. "You don't seem to have a fever."

"It's just an upset stomach," he replies. Although it is hard to hold back the joy of finding the phone, he forces a pained expression.

"Maybe a pleasant afternoon by the Seine—"

Julien shakes his head and pulls his face into a frown. "I think not; but don't let me spoil your afternoon. You go. Perhaps if I stay here and rest I'll feel better by evening."

She gives a lighthearted laugh. "I have no desire to go without you. I'll stay and keep you company."

"No, really. You'll only make me feel bad if—"

She leans across the table and touches her finger to his lips. "Not another word. My mind is made up." She stands then leans down and covers his mouth with hers.

FOR NEARLY THREE HOURS JULIEN lies on the bed. He is restless and itchy to move but cannot. Brigitte is beside him, her leg atop his and her shoulder pressed against his arm. She haphazardly flips through the pages of a magazine, not reading, just glancing at a page or two then moving on.

Halfway through she stops and squeals, "Ooh, look at this!" She holds the page open for him to see.

It is a red dress worn by a model skinnier than Brigitte.

"Wouldn't I love to have this…" she says, sighing.

Julien eyes the page. "On you this dress would look better than on the model."

She turns to him, her eyes sparkling with the delight of his words. "Do you honestly think so?"

"Yes." He nods. "If we had a bit more money in the box, I would say go right now and buy that dress."

"At one-hundred and fifty euros?" She laughs. "You are much too generous." She leans over and traces her tongue along the edge of his ear. "It was only a thought. I don't really need such a fancy dress."

"Yes, you do. I want you to have it."

"But the money—"

"We have a suitcase filled with telephones; that is money enough. This afternoon you can take them to the buyer and collect what we are owed."

She looks at him wide-eyed. "Alone? You want me to go alone to the buyer?"

"Why not?" he says casually, making it sound as if it were not a matter of concern. "I trust you."

"But I've never—"

"The buyer knows you. He's seen you with me often enough."

"I'm not so sure…"

"Go," he says laughingly. "I will sleep for a while, and when you get back we will celebrate with dinner at the café."

"And tomorrow I can buy the dress?"

He nods. "Yes, tomorrow you can buy the dress."

AS SOON AS BRIGITTE IS out of the apartment, Julien plugs in the charger cord and begins to try different passcodes. The apartment he and Max shared was in building number 4, so he tries 4444. Incorrect password. He is certain Max's birthday is in September so he tries every date. Still incorrect password. He even tries his own birthday, but still no luck. When he hears Brigitte's key in the lock, he powers off the phone and slides it back into his pocket.

Now that she is no longer watching him, he will be freer to come and go. It is too late to go back to the buyer today, but tomorrow afternoon he will go. At four o'clock when the buyer arrives at the spot, Julien will be there waiting. The buyer has ways of unlocking a phone.

BRIGITTE COMES INTO THE BEDROOM wearing a smile. She waves a fistful of bills in the air.

"Three hundred and forty euros," she says happily. She goes to the closet, pushes the box of books to the side, pries up the loose floorboard and removes the metal box where the money is kept.

She adds her bills to the stack then counts them. "One thousand four hundred and ninety."

"That should keep us for a while." Julien gives a nod toward the stack of bills. "Take out one hundred and fifty euros to buy the dress and give me one hundred for my pocket."

Brigitte does as she is told, then lowers the box back into its hiding place, presses the floorboard down and slides the carton of books back into place.

JULIEN

Brigitte has been watching me every minute of every day. She knows me too well. She expected me to search the suitcase for the phone, which is why she wouldn't let me out of her sight. Now things have changed. She is thinking only of the dress and does not realize I have found her hiding place.

Twice I've taken the phone into the bathroom hoping I might try a few more codes, but she sits only a few steps away. Even though she is naïve and easily fooled she would quickly enough recognize the sound of a cell phone, so I dared not turn it on. Knowing Brigitte as I do, I assure you a locked door would not stop her from entering.

Now that she has given up watching me, it will be much easier to slip away. I will say wait until afternoon to shop for the dress, and while she is out I will pay a visit to the buyer. He will have no trouble unlocking Max's phone.

I don't know what I expect to find, but still I have to look.

Since last Sunday I have been unable to stop thinking about Max. Looking back on our year together, I remember that it was a very good time in my life.

Max has a different way of looking at things. Times when we couldn't even afford a bottle of cheap wine, she'd laugh and claim it was

184

only temporary. "Be patient," she'd say. "One day you'll be a rich and famous artist with paintings hanging in the d'Orsay." The funny thing is that sometimes I'd actually believe it.

On the last day when I watched her walk away at the airport I knew I'd never again see her, and it was okay. I told myself it's better this way. In a month or so we'll forget each other and move on to living the lives we're supposed to live. Max's was far different than mine. She had expectations I could never live up to. Back then I was absolutely certain of all this, but on Sunday when I looked into her face I began to wonder if I hadn't made a terrible mistake.

Brigitte and Max are as different as night and day. Brigitte has no expectations. She knows the worst of me and loves me despite it. The truth is we are better suited for one another. Her soul is almost a mirror image of my own. Neither of us expects much out of life. We take what we can and be content with it.

Perhaps I should leave things as they are, but I can't bring myself to do it. I keep wondering if maybe, just maybe, I could be the man Max believes I am.

MEETING THE BUYER

On Friday morning when Brigitte wakes she is already aglow.

"Today I go to buy the red dress," she reminds Julien. "Will you come with me?"

He gives a labored sigh. "I think not. Such shops bore me. Better you go alone; then you can take time to search through the dresses. Perhaps you will find one you prefer over the red one."

Brigitte laughs. "Never. That dress was made for me; you said so yourself."

"True." Julien nods. "But still you will have fun looking. You might find a little something else you want. A scarf perhaps? Or colored sandals?"

The thought of something extra pleases Brigitte. She smiles and swings her feet to the floor. "I'll go now and hurry back. We can spend the afternoon—"

"Not so fast," he says and tugs her back into the bed. "Are you not going to show your appreciation?"

Julien needs to keep her there until it is close to four o'clock. That is when the buyer will be at the meeting place. Although she

186

no longer watches him like a hawk, Brigitte is clingy and wants to tag along regardless of where he is going. If she is not here, it will be easier to leave and there will be no questions.

She drops back onto the bed then leans forward and lowers her face to his. With her mouth pursed in a pretend pout, she says, "Didn't I already say you are the most generous man in all the world?"

"Words are cheap," Julien laughingly replies.

"And so..." She teases her fingers along the side of his face, down his neck and onto his chest. "You think I should make love to you as payment for the dress?"

"No, I think you should make love to me because you want to." Julien says this because he knows it is what he must say to keep Brigitte occupied. He would just as soon she go back to sleep, read a magazine or dabble around in the kitchen; but to say such a thing would only trigger an argument.

He glances at the clock. It is only ten. Six hours until the buyer will be at the meeting place.

THE NEXT TIME JULIEN LOOKS at the clock it is not yet noon. It seems the hours move as slowly as an old man with a sack of bricks tied to his back.

"I want to do something," Brigitte complains. "I'm tired of lying in bed."

"Then go make coffee and fix me something to eat."

She grudgingly climbs from the bed, but instead of turning toward the kitchen she stands at the window and pushes back the draperies.

"Look at the blue of the sky," she says. "This day is telling us to be outside."

Julien pinches up the left side of his mouth and gives her a look of skepticism.

"I hear only the grumble of my hungry stomach," he says.

"If I make sandwiches will you come with me to the Tulleries for a picnic?"

He frowns at the thought.

"Please," she begs. "It's only for a few hours. We'll sit on the grass and have a nice lunch. Afterward I'll go to buy the dress and you can come home to rest those lazy bones."

At this thought Julien smiles. The timing would be right. "Okay. But we will leave in one hour. I want time to shower and dress."

"For that you need an hour?" She heaves an exaggerated sigh. "Such a slowpoke."

"No more complaining, or I'll go back to bed!"

"Okay, okay." She laughs and prances off toward the kitchen.

WHEN JULIEN COMES FROM THE bedroom, he is clean-shaven and wearing his good black trousers.

"Rather dressed up for a picnic, aren't you?" Brigitte says.

"With such a fancy new dress, I thought that later you might want to go to the restaurant for dinner."

"The restaurant?" she says. "Not the café?"

Julien knows Brigitte only too well; she is a woman who can be pushed into nothing but tricked into almost anything. "Of course if you would prefer I change..."

"No, no," she says. "I like the thought of the restaurant." She gives him a devilish grin and adds, "I will wear a lipstick as red as the dress."

THEY HAVE BARELY SETTLED ON the grassy lawn near the fountain when Julien begins checking his watch. He is anxious to have lunch over with so that when it is a quarter of four he can hurry off. If he didn't know better he would swear Brigitte is toying with him, moving slowly when he wants her to hurry and ready to dart off when he is stalling for time.

As she unwraps the baguettes, Brigitte notices the way Julien drums the fingers of one hand against the other. "You seem jumpy as a flea. What's wrong?"

"Nothing," he says, "I'm just hungry." His words are sharp, and threaded with impatience.

Brigitte angrily thumps the wrapped baguette into his lap. "Are you so hungry you can't relax and just enjoy being with me?"

For a while there is no more conversation, but Brigitte's anger is short-lived. Before long she moves on to idle chatter about things Julien has no interest in hearing. There is talk of a cooking class at the church on Rue Monge and a visit from her sister at the end of the summer.

As Julien watches the hands of his watch tick off the minutes, he tries to appear interested. Every so often he nods or repeats a word or two of what she has said, but his thoughts are elsewhere. He is remembering the afternoons spent with Max in this very same spot.

When it is finally three-thirty, he reminds Brigitte of the dress.

"I'm in no hurry," she says. "The shop is open until seven."

Julien stands and stretches. "Well, you can go look around or stay here if you want, but if we are going to the restaurant tonight I need to go home and take a short nap." Even as he says this he worries that she will latch onto his arm and follow him home.

She doesn't. Brigitte is happy with the thought of browsing through the rack of dresses and perhaps buying a new nail polish to match the red dress.

They walk to the edge of the park together; then she turns

toward the Champs Elysées and he walks in the direction of Rue Racine. Once she is out of sight, he crosses over and heads for the metro station.

It is twenty minutes before four.

WHEN THE BUYER WALKS INTO the darkened bistro, Julien is already waiting.

"I need a favor," he says.

"I don't do favors," the buyer replies. "Unless you've got something to sell, get out of here."

"This is personal. I just need you to unlock a phone," Julien says. "I'll pay for your time."

The buyer sticks out a bony hand. "Let's see what you've got."

Julien pulls Max's phone from his pocket and passes it across the table. The buyer peels the pink case from the phone and tosses it back.

"Get rid of this," he says. "Shit like this is how people get caught."

Julien pockets the case and waits.

The buyer tries two or three codes then looks up. "Fifty euros."

"Fifty euros just to unlock the phone?"

The buyer nods. "Cash up front. Yes or no?"

Julien reaches into his pocket, pulls out a handful of bills and peels off five ten-euro notes. "Do it," he says and hands the buyer the money.

The bony hand pockets both the phone and the cash. "Monday, four o'clock."

Julien gasps. "Monday? I can't wait until Monday. I need it sooner."

The buyer points a warning finger across the table. "Keep your voice down. I'm not here weekends; you know that. You want sooner than Monday it's an extra hundred."

Julien digs into his pocket but can only come up with seventy euros. He hands the money to the buyer. "Trust me on the balance; you know I'm good for it."

"I trust nobody," the buyer says. "Tomorrow morning, ten o'clock. Be here and have the money, or you lose the phone."

"I'll be here." Julien stands and starts toward the door. From the corner of his eye he sees a young girl waiting. Before he steps out onto the street, she slides into the seat across from the buyer.

This is how it always is. The buyer comes at four, sits at the table furthest from the window, has a single glass of burgundy and leaves at five. He does all of his business during that hour. Where he comes from and where he goes, no one knows.

Although the buyer says he trusts no one, Julien wonders if the buyer himself can be trusted.

A Visit to Versailles

On Friday morning as Andrew pulls out of the small parking lot in back of Le Maison d'hote Max turns, takes one last look at the large stone house and gives a wistful sigh.

"Last night was so lovely," she says. "I only wish..."

"Wish what?" Andrew asks.

The answer she gives is not the full truth of what she is thinking. "I wish I'd brought a change of clothes and some makeup. The only thing I had in my bag was a comb and lip gloss."

He glances over, and his eyes study her face. "You don't need anything else; you're beautiful just as you are."

Max plants a kiss on the tips of her finger, then reaches across and touches it to his cheek. "Mmmuah," she says as if she is transferring the kiss. There is a moment of hesitation; then she adds, "Thank you for making last night easy for me."

"Easy?"

"You know what I mean," she says. "Being together in a room like that...well, a lot of men would have pushed for more. You didn't, and that was very sweet."

A smile curls the corner of Andrew's mouth. "Don't think I didn't want to," he says playfully. "It was a test of my willpower."

"Mine too," Max replies.

His smile broadens. He reaches across the seat and affectionately squeezes her hand.

THE PALACE AT VERSAILLES IS only 65 kilometers from Giverny and Andrew has never been there, so they decide to make a day of it. Any trace of last night's storm is long gone. The day is bright and the sun warm against their shoulders.

Andrew again lowers the convertible roof, and the soft breeze ruffles their hair. "Too much?"

Max shakes her head. "I like it."

Instead of taking the highway he travels the back roads that weave in and out of small villages. Along the way there are fields of wildflowers, stone churches and farms bordering patches of waist-high wheat.

Max has an eye for detail, and twice they stop for a better look at an age-old building. The first time it is an abandoned farmhouse. The door is missing, so they step inside and look around. The rooms smell of dampness and nothing has been left behind, so after a few minutes they move on.

Their second stop is a small church set back from the road. Max steps up onto the stone ledge and touches her hand to the stained glass window.

"The man who created this was old," she says. "In his last years of life."

Andrew gives her a quizzical look. "How do you know that?"

"His pain is still here in the pieces of glass. See this mark?" She points to a tiny nick in the edge of Mary's robe. "When he cut this piece, he had tremors and his hand was shaking."

Andrew looks at her wide-eyed. "Can you do like Annie does—know the thoughts of other people?"

"Read minds?" She laughs. "Hardly. But I can often feel the aura people have left behind."

"Amazing."

"Not really," Max says. "There's always some tiny detail that tells me about the person who created the piece of art or lived there. Feeling the aura is not a supernatural thing, it's just zeroing in on that one tiny clue and then imagining myself in that time and place. Try it."

"Me?" Andrew says. "I could never—"

"Just try it," she urges. "The next time you see something that piques your interest just touch it, then close your eyes and see what happens."

Andrew gives her a devilish grin. "Okay," he says then reaches over, places his hand on her forehead and closes his eyes.

"It doesn't work with people," she says and playfully brushes his hand away.

Feigning disappointment Andrew asks, "Why not?"

"A building doesn't hide its scars and years of wear; only people do. Secrets of the past can sometimes be painful. Hiding them doesn't change anything, but people usually feel better if no one else can see their scars."

As they turn back to the car Max thinks of her own past and wonders if she will ever willingly share her own ugly secrets.

BY THE TIME THEY REACH Versailles it is past noon, so they stop in the village and search for a place to eat. Andrew parks the car and they walk. Two blocks down they find La Table Rouge and go in. It is a small café with only a few of the bright red tables still open.

The proprietor, a robust man with a white apron tied around his waist, motions to a table along the wall and waves them over.

"Merci," Max says as she slides into the chair. This is the type of place where there is no menu; today's dishes are written on a chalkboard.

"Take your time," the owner says and disappears back into the kitchen.

When he returns to take their order, he brings two small glasses of a sparkling pear wine.

"For the newlyweds," he says and gives a broad smile.

"Oh...um," Max stammers, but before she has time to say anything more Andrew smiles and replies, "Merci."

When they are again alone she whispers. "He thought we were—"

"I know," Andrew says with a mischievous smile. "But if we corrected the mistake he'd be embarrassed; this way he hangs on to the pleasure of what he did."

Max smiles at the thought and mentally adds another item to the growing list of Andrew's attributes. This one reads, "Considerate of others."

WHEN THEY ARRIVE AT THE palace it is crowded, as it always is. Max stops at the front desk and grabs two English-language audio guides. She has been here twice before, but it has been over three years and there is much she does not remember. They pass through the lounge area then enter a room that houses a model of the palace and its grounds.

She hands one of the audio guides to Andrew. They both slide the ear buds into place and click the devices on.

"The Palace of Versailles was originally a hunting lodge," the narrator says, "but in sixteen twenty-three, Louis the thirteenth..."

Andrew nudges her. "Are you getting any sound?"

She nods. "Aren't you?"

He shakes his head.

She pulls the earphones out and hands her audio guide to him. "Try mine."

He pops the earphones in then nods.

"Okay, you use them," Max says. "I've been here before so I don't need to—"

He again shakes his head then pulls one earphone out and hands it to her. "We'll share."

He reaches over and tucks the second earphone into her ear then loops his arm around her shoulder. This is how they spend the afternoon, with one audio guide tying the two of them together.

On the tour they move through grand ballrooms with windows overlooking the gardens, the king's bedroom with its massive bed and velvet draperies, the equally grand queen's bedroom and the much-touted Hall of Mirrors, but the thing Andrew remembers most is the sharing of earphones.

BY THE TIME THEY ARRIVE back in Paris it is near dark. Andrew returns the car, and they go to dinner. It is late, but they are in no hurry. They linger with a cocktail before dinner and coffee afterwards.

It is after midnight when he walks her back to the Hotel Vendome. They pass through the lobby and go back to where the elevator is. She stands with her back to the wall, and he faces her.

For a moment there is only silence; then they both speak at once.

"Thank you—" she says.

"Tomorrow—" he says.

They both laugh.

"You first." He gestures and gives her a playful smile.

"I was going to say thank you for such a wonderful two days." She looks up and directly into the soft gray of his eyes. "I can't remember when I've had a nicer time."

"Me too," Andrew says. He leans forward with his hand braced against the wall and his face tilted down towards hers. "Tomorrow at ten?"

She starts to answer, but there is a lump in her throat. She swallows hard and nods. Finally the words come. "That would be—"

The word "wonderful" never comes, because he covers her mouth with his. The kiss is long and sweet.

When he releases her she feels a little dreamy and a lot confused.

He pushes the button, and the elevator door slides open. She steps in and looks back at him. As the door is closing she sees him mouth the word, *Tomorrow*.

The Discovery

When Julien leaves the buyer his mood is as black as a storm cloud. He has no love for the buyer as it is, but now his dislike has bubbled into hatred.

"Played me for a fool is what he did," Julien grumbles as he crosses over Rue Emireau. He ignores the passersby and talks to himself. "He saw I was anxious to get the phone unlocked, so he stuck it to me."

Sucker.

One hundred and fifty euros to do something that likely takes five, maybe ten minutes. Outrageous.

Instead of taking the metro, Julien walks. He tries to shake the anger loose, but with every step it grows bigger. Meaner. Over the past year he has given the buyer hundreds of phones and stacks of credit cards. That should count for something. *Once the phone is unlocked, what is there to be gained anyway? A telephone number? An address here in Paris? Then what?*

Julien knows with Max there's only the slimmest chance she'll take him back. Brigitte is a sure thing. With Brigitte his life is easy; he has only to nod, and she lifts the phone or wallet from a stranger's pocket. With Brigitte there are no expectations. She takes what he gives and is happy with it.

With Max there are expectations; too many expectations. Marriage. Family. Work. With her life would be a tar pit of responsibilities, and his life would forever be changed. She offers him nothing, and yet he cannot chase her from his mind.

Julien sees a loose button dropped on the sidewalk, and he kicks it aside with a vengeance. It is something to vent his anger on.

HE IS HALFWAY TO THE apartment when the anger building inside him explodes, and he turns. *Screw it*, he thinks and heads back to the bistro. He is going to tell the buyer to give back his money and forget about unlocking the phone. His stride is long and his face chiseled in a look of determination.

In time he'll forget Max. He did it once before; he can do it again. He thinks about tonight's dinner in the restaurant and tries to picture Brigitte in the red dress, but what he sees is Max's face last Sunday morning. This only angers him more.

As much as he wants to hate Max, he can't. He is still in love with her.

HE CROSSES BACK OVER RUE Emireau and storms into the bistro. The table is empty, the buyer gone.

Julien turns to the waiter and grabs the front of his shirt. "Where is he?"

The waiter, a small man with the frail bones of a child, trembles. "Where is who, monsieur?"

"The buyer! The man who was just sitting at this table!"

The waiter gives a helpless shrug. "He is a stranger, monsieur. He comes, he goes, but where he does not say."

Julien releases his hold on the frightened waiter and storms out. He knows this is true. The buyer is a shadow that comes for one hour then disappears into nothingness. His money is gone. The only thing he can do is wait until tomorrow, pay the additional thirty euros and take possession of Max's phone.

Hopefully it will be worth all the aggravation.

Julien again turns toward the apartment building and walks. This time his steps are slow and his shoulders sloped forward.

IT IS AFTER SIX WHEN he arrives home, and Brigitte is already at the apartment.

"I thought you said you needed to take a nap," she growls. The sound of anger is like an electrical current running through her words.

"I do," Julien replies and heads for the bedroom.

Brigitte is right behind him, trailing so close her toes bang up against his heels. "Where were you?" Her voice is higher now, not screeching but on the verge of it.

"I went for a walk," Julien answers; then he plops down on the bed.

She leans over him, her nose a hair's breadth from his. "Liar! You went to meet that girl, didn't you?"

"What girl?"

"You know what girl!" She pushes her hands into his chest. "The one from Sunday. The one with the pink phone."

Julien shakes her off and stands. "Stop screaming!" he yells, but his voice is louder than hers.

Seconds later Madame Chastain bangs on the ceiling.

He lowers his voice and then says, "I told you I have no interest in her—"

"Liar! You found the phone and took it to her!"

"Brigitte, listen..." He reaches for her, but she backs away.

"Don't touch me! I already know! You took the phone from under the mattress!"

Several thumps come from the ceiling below, and Madame Chastain hollers that she will call the police if they don't quiet down.

"Call them if you want!" Brigitte yells back. "I don't give a crap!"

"Please, Brigitte..." Julien again reaches for her, and again she backs away.

"Do you think me so stupid that I don't know when you lie?" She turns away from him. "I know," she says bitterly, "but I put up with it."

"Okay, you're right," Julien admits. "I did take the phone, but I put it in with all the others you took to the buyer. I was going to keep it, but I didn't."

"Ha!" Brigitte tosses her head and glares over her shoulder. "Even that is a lie! The buyer counted the phones in front of me, and there was no pink phone!"

Julien remembers the case in his pocket. "I took the cover off," he says. "I told you that damn pink cover was too identifiable."

"Liar."

"It's the truth. Look, I still have the cover." He pulls the pink case from his pocket. "I was going to toss it in a trash bin far from here but forgot."

Brigitte doesn't answer; she doesn't even turn around. She stands there silent, her back to Julien.

"Please, Brigitte baby, you've got to believe me. You know how much I love you. How can you not know?"

She gives an almost imperceptible shrug but doesn't turn around.

Julien comes up behind her, wraps his arms around her narrow shoulders, and whispers in her ear. "I love you, Brigitte; you know I do. I'll give you anything you want. Please, baby..."

In time he wears away her resistance and she turns, offering up her mouth.

AFTERWARD THEY MAKE LOVE, AND it lasts long into the night. He whispers of how much he loves her, and Brigitte believes him because it is what she wants to believe.

When she falls asleep, Julien is still awake. He is thinking of tomorrow.

THROUGHOUT THE NIGHT JULIEN IS restless. Several times he wakes and then struggles to get back to sleep. When the first light of morning is in the sky, he climbs from the bed and pulls on his clothes. He moves slowly and silently, moving like a shadow so he will not disturb Brigitte. She is a sound sleeper, but still he cannot afford to take chances.

When she groans and twists her body from one position to another, he presses his back to the wall and remains hidden.

Before he leaves he must get another thirty euros for the buyer. Lifting the floorboard in the closet would be too noisy, so he slides Brigitte's purse from atop the nightstand and takes the bills she has in her wallet. Sixty euros. It is enough.

Leaving the apartment he closes the door softly behind him. There will be hell to pay when he returns, but that is something to deal with when the time comes.

For now he can think only about meeting the buyer and the information he will find on Max's phone.

BRIGITTE

J ulien was gone when I woke this morning. I knew then that last night was nothing but more of his lies.

I am worn weary of lies and stealing, of ducking into doorways when we see a policeman. I want a life like my sister has. Elena works in a bakery surrounded by the smell of fresh bread and sweet rolls. At the end of the day she comes home to a husband who offers her hands dirty from work, not filled with money from other people's pockets.

Hers is a simple life, not one of fancy dresses and evenings at the café. But she is happy. Eli is not a handsome man, but he has a good heart and a warm smile. Elena never questions whether or not he loves her. She knows he does, because he is always there. If I so much as blink an eye, Julien is gone. Off chasing another woman or perhaps looking for greener pastures.

I know loving him has made a fool of me, but I am neither stupid nor blind. I saw how he looked at that woman. It was as if he were standing naked before her, stripped of all pretenses and left with only an apology to offer.

Not once has he ever looked at me that way. Not once. If he did I would follow him to the ends of the earth. I would continue to steal for *him and lay down my life if need be. I would damn my soul to eternal hell for Julien if he loved me; but he does not.*

This morning I took the suitcase from beneath the bed and packed my clothes in it. I left the red dress behind, because where I am going I will not need such a dress.

When Julien returns, if he returns, he will find the money from the box and me both gone. He will no doubt rant and rave, swearing that I have taken everything and left nothing for him. That is not the truth. I have left behind something far more valuable than stolen money. I have left behind a large piece of my heart.

This morning I promised myself that once I walk out the door, I will no longer think of Julien.

I want to believe this, but I know it is a lie. I am a woman who has grown used to living with lies, so I lie—even to myself.

THE MESSAGES

Julien is at the bistro a half-hour before it opens. He sits on a bench in the park and waits. At seven-thirty a portly man with a ring of keys dangling from his belt comes and unlocks the door. It is not the waiter of yesterday evening but more likely the owner.

After a few moments Julien crosses the park and enters the bistro. The man behind the counter now has an apron tied around his waist.

"Coffee?" he asks.

"Double," Julien grunts and moves toward the back.

The morning is just getting started, and most of the chairs are still upended on the tables. When Julien reaches the table in the far corner he yanks a chair down and sits where the buyer usually sits, facing the door with his back to the wall. It is a way of gaining the upper hand, a way of showing his disdain for the hefty price the buyer charges.

It is not yet eight o'clock. Two hours to wait. The buyer is never early, never late. Like some sort of pompous king, he sets the rules and forces those who want to do business with him to abide by them. This thought rankles Julien.

The owner comes, sets a large cup of coffee on the table and says nothing. Julien could care less about him. The man is a peon. Julien's anger is reserved for the buyer.

Today he will say something. He will say the price for unlocking a cell phone is outrageous and demand half the money back. Although he is angry, he is also clever enough to wait until he has Max's phone in his hand. Once he sees it is unlocked, that's when he will tell the buyer the truth of what is on his mind.

Julien drops a single lump of sugar into his coffee and stirs it. He thinks back to Sunday and pictures the look on Max's face. Shock, yes, but there was something more. When he said "Later at the café," she nodded. She came that night, he is almost certain of it.

True, she is a woman with expectations, but perhaps that is what he needs to spur him on to all he is capable of achieving. He made good money selling small sketches that took minutes to do; perhaps if he were to stand at the easel and paint, as she wanted him to... He imagines a gallery showing and smiles at the thought.

Of course, there is the problem of Brigitte. She is a feisty little tart with an uncontrollable temper. Julien doubts he can just slip away from her; she is clever enough to track him down. Perhaps he should offer an excuse. Something to placate her until the anger dies down.

He decides to say he will be gone for just a month or two. He will claim he is going to Chartres to care for an ailing cousin. That is a believable enough story. He will give Brigitte two hundred euros and tell her to keep the apartment; that way if things do not work out, he can come back.

Confident that he has the best of plans, Julien leans back in the chair and signals for another coffee. He checks his watch. Five minutes after nine. It is now less than an hour. The minutes crawl by, and as he waits he downs three more of the double espressos.

When the long hand of his watch ticks past the hour Julien becomes edgy.

It is not like the buyer to be late, yet it is already one minute past ten. Nervously drumming his fingers on the table, he thinks back to the conversation of yesterday. Ten o'clock. He is certain the buyer said ten o'clock.

Julien stands, walks to the front of the bistro and steps out onto the street. There is no sign of the buyer. He looks both ways then grumbles, "Son of a bitch." Seething, he stomps back inside and plops down at the table.

He downs the last few drops of coffee and tries to think. What if the buyer doesn't show up? What then? There's no way to get in touch with him, to get either the phone or his money back. The thought of being suckered rises like the steam of a teakettle. Julien is just about to boil over when he finally sees the buyer come through the door.

With his eyes narrowed and his face set in a look of defiance, he waits until the buyer nears the table then says, "You're late!"

Without saying a word, the buyer turns and starts back toward the door.

Julien jumps up. "Wait!" he shouts and hurries after the man. He stretches his arm and catches the buyer's shoulder.

The buyer turns, his eyes as cold and hard as ice. "Do I know you?"

"Of course you do," Julien says. "We were to meet here." Too much caffeine has jangled his nerves, and the sound of desperation is threaded through his voice. "You're supposed to deliver a phone, and I'm to give you another thirty euros."

"Fifty euros," the buyer says.

"Yesterday it was thirty."

"Fifty," the buyer repeats. "Yesterday was before you gave me attitude."

"I'm sorry," Julien mumbles. "Please—"

"Fifty. You've got ten seconds to decide."

Julien reaches into his pocket and pulls out the bills. After he hands the buyer the fifty, he is given the phone.

"Don't come back," the buyer says.

Julien looks at him quizzically. "What do you mean, don't come back?"

"This is it," the buyer says. "Hotheads like you have trouble written all over them. We're through doing business."

With that the buyer turns and walks out the door.

"You think I give a shit?" Julien mutters. "Assholes like you are a dime a dozen." He goes to the counter, hands the owner his last ten-euro note and walks out the door.

Crossing over to the park, Julien returns to the bench where he sat earlier. He turns the phone on and waits while it loads. A number 3 pops up over the icon for messages.

Julien clicks on it and begins to read.

The most recent message is from someone named Annie. She asks if Max is still at Hotel Vendome and whether or not she has found Julien. *She came here looking for me. A good sign.*

He moves onto the second message. It is from a Mark Treadway. He says Doctor Kelly's construction is going well and that a check is in the mail. He also mentions that he has another new client for Max. *She is obviously making money,* Julien thinks. *So much the better.*

The third message is again from Annie. It says if Max has not yet found Julien she should try not to be too upset.

He smiles. She is as good as his. He will say what she wants to hear, and she will fall into his arms as she did before. Again his thoughts drift back to Sunday and now he can see it clearly. The look on Max's face was not shock, it was adoration. She is still in love with him.

JULIEN ARRIVES AT THE HOTEL Vendome just minutes after Max and Andrew have left. When the desk clerk says there is no answer in her room, Julien says he will wait. He moves to the small group of leather chairs in the corner of the lobby, sits down and picks a magazine from the table.

⚭

THIS IS THEIR LAST FULL day in Paris, so Max takes Andrew on a walking tour. They weave in and out of narrow cobblestoned streets and stroll the wide boulevards. She shows him the buildings that fired her love of architecture and points out tiny details, details that are often too small to garner notice: a cornerstone dating back to the 1700s, a chandelier of rose-colored glass, a twist of wrought iron, a cherub with part of the face chipped away.

Andrew listens as if she is speaking the word of God, and he cannot take his eyes from her face. He delights in the way she touches a stone as tenderly as she would a child and how her skin reflects the sunlight when she tilts her face to point out a row of pitched roofs.

In time they leave the Latin Quarter and take the metro over to the fashionable right bank. They stroll the Champs Elysées and stop for lunch at the Renault, an outdoor restaurant with pink placemats and napkins tied with ribbon.

As they linger at the table with coffee and a small plate of pastries, Andrew says, "I came here thinking this would be an ordinary business trip." He hesitates then adds, "But being with you has turned it into the best vacation ever."

He stretches his arm across the table and lifts Max's hand into his.

She looks at him, her eyes soft and gentle. "I've enjoyed it also.

209

You've been..." She is going to say her knight in shining armor but she decides such a phrase is too corny, so she replaces it with, "A life saver."

Life saver is good, but Andrew is hoping for more. "When we get back to Virginia, let's continue this."

The "this" of his statement is understood. Max knows he is referring to the relationship that has blossomed.

"I'd like that," she says. "Very much."

Without taking his eyes from her face, he lifts her hand to his mouth and drops a kiss into her palm. He then folds her fingers back and says, "Hold on to that. It's yours to keep."

The moment is so special Max intends to hold on to it for a very long time. She takes her closed fist, moves it to the spot where her heart is, then opens her hand and presses it to her chest.

"This is where it will stay," she says.

Andrew smiles. If he had any doubts that he is falling in love with her, they are now gone.

After lunch they visit the Arc d' Triomphe, then head for the Tulleries Gardens to stroll along the pathways. When the sun is low in the sky, they cross the Pont des Arts bridge and start toward the Eiffel Tower. Andrew tells Max he has planned a sweet surprise for their last evening.

"I think you're going to like it," he says.

"The suspense is killing me," Max replies.

When they reach the Eiffel Tower they circle around to the far side—to the entrance that houses the private elevator going up to Le Jules Verne.

Max gasps. "Are you serious?"

This is the reaction Andrew hopes for. "Have you been here before?"

"Gosh, no," she replies. "This place was way beyond my budget."

"Good," he says. "I wanted it to be something special, sort of a first for us."

Max tilts her head so she is eye-to-eye with him. "We've had a lot of firsts, and they've all been pretty special."

A maître'd takes their name, confirms the reservation, then escorts them up in the elevator. They sit at a table alongside the window and gaze out as the last rays of sunlight filters across the landscape of Paris.

"From here the city looks so beautiful," Max says.

"From where I'm sitting everything looks beautiful," Andrew replies.

The room seems to be lit by only the candles on the table, and the sound is as hushed as a lullaby. The waiters move silently and are almost invisible unless there is another goblet of wine to be poured or dish to be served.

As the sky grows dark, they linger with coffee and a chocolate soufflé; when night settles over the city, the tower is lit with a golden glow. At the stroke of the nine o'clock hour, a trail of sparkling lights flitters up and down the tower. Max watches with the wonder of a child, and her eyes reflect the sparkle of the lights. The table Andrew has selected sits in the center of it all; he smiles knowing this was indeed a good choice.

When they leave the restaurant, they walk back to the Hotel Vendome. It is a long walk but seems too short. He walks with his arm circling her waist, and she curls herself into him as if she is meant to be there.

JULIEN IS STILL SITTING IN the corner chair. He has left it only for a few moments at a time—long enough to grab another container of coffee or use the toilet. For twelve hours he has watched the door, waiting for her return.

He sees them as they step into the lobby. The man with his arm around her like she belongs to him. The two of them walking together as he once did with her.

They pass him by as if he doesn't exist.

Julien stands and calls out her name. "Maxine!"

She turns quickly; her face drains of color. "Julien?"

Andrew looks at the stranger and then turns back to Max. "Julien? Is this the Julien that..." The remainder of his question hangs in the air.

Max nods then stumbles through an introduction. "Andrew," she says warily, "meet Julien Marceau. Julien, Andrew Steen."

The men shake hands, but it is the handshake of two boxers readying themselves for battle.

Andrew gives a slight nod.

Julien doesn't do even that. He turns to Max and says, "I've got to talk to you."

For a long moment Max stands there and says nothing, her expression stony and the muscles in her back rigid.

"Why now?" she finally asks. "What are you looking for this time, Julien?"

Andrew notices that she doesn't say no. She is hesitant, but she doesn't turn him away; there is still a question in her mind.

"Please," Julien begs, "it's important. There are things I have to say."

Andrew looks down at Max. "I'd better go. You and Julien obviously have things to talk about."

Before she can deny this, Andrew turns and walks away. There is no kiss goodbye, only the back of his broad shoulders disappearing into the night.

ANDREW STEEN

Maybe walking away is the dumbest thing I've ever done in my entire life, but the truth is I had no choice.

Yes, I love Max; I've come to realize that more with every minute we spend together. But loving someone doesn't guarantee they'll love you back. I want her to love me and I'll do anything in my power to win that love, but I won't take it by default.

I knew from the start that she came here looking for this man, but I thought maybe by now she had forgotten him. Unfortunately I don't think she has.

The instant he called her name, her expression changed. I can't say what was going through her head. Shock, maybe? Anger? Love?

There was a moment when she could have turned her back and walked away, but she didn't. She waited and let him reach out for her.

In the courtroom I have all too often seen the faces of desperation, and this Julien had that same look on his face. Perhaps he wants Max as much as I do. It's impossible to know why he's here or what he wants.

Him I don't care about.

But where Max is concerned, this much I know: there can be no "us" until she has rid her heart of "him."

THE CONVERSATION

As soon as Andrew is gone, Julien grabs Max's hand and holds it to his heart.

"Feel the pounding," he says. "It's caused by a fear of losing you."

Max looks away, not allowing her eyes to meet his. "Why are you here, Julien? I have nothing more for you to steal."

Julien's face takes on a look of shock. "Mon dieu! You think I would steal from you?"

"You did already," Max says. "You and your girlfriend took my phone, my wallet and the last bit of dignity I had."

"Not me!" he exclaims. "The little witch, she is the one. I knew nothing of what she was doing. Only later I learned, and then it was too late." He heaves a great sigh as if this thought burdens his heart.

He pulls the phone from his pocket and hands it to her. "I came here to return this." He stops in the middle of his words and focuses his eyes on the floor. "I am ashamed to say the money she has kept."

Max slides the phone into her pocket and turns away. "Why should I believe anything you say? You've lied to me before, and—"

"I was a fool," Julien cuts in. "I was a fool to let you go, but I was a fool in love. I thought what I was doing was right. I had nothing to offer and believed you would be better off without me."

As Julien speaks tears roll from his eyes, and Max sees this.

"You could have let me know," she says. "You could have sent an email or found some way to contact me. Maybe if you would have said something..."

Julien sees this crack in her defenses. "Let's go to your room, some place private where we can—"

"Absolutely not."

"Then come and sit with me. There is so much we need to talk about." He takes her hand and tugs her to the corner of the lobby.

She sits in one chair, and he sits across from her.

"Your being here is a bad idea," she says. "I'm going home tomorrow—"

He drops forward and falls on his knees, his head in her lap. "Please, Maxine, don't go. Now that I've found you I can't bear to lose you again."

He utters a sob-like sound, and Max feels the quivering of his shoulders. There is a part of her that wants to reach down and comfort him, cradle his head in her hands and say that she also knows the pain of the past three years. But she holds back.

"Please don't do this," she says. "It's too late, too much has happened—"

He lifts his head and looks into her eyes. "It should never be too late for a man who is truly in love."

His words are like opium, a drug that poisons with visions of beauty.

He tells Max he has left the little witch, that he wants to start anew, make a life together. At some point his words start to sound truthful. Perhaps because they are the words she has waited so long to hear.

He pleads with her not to leave, saying he still loves her, that he has never stopped loving her.

The three years of longing are there, just beneath Max's skin, but now they are mixed with other emotions. A voice in the back of her mind whispers, *Once a liar, always a liar.*

After almost two hours of listening to his pleas and promises, she pushes him away.

"You should go, Julien," she says. "There is nothing more for us to talk about."

"You're wrong," he says. "I know I've hurt you, but that's in the past. I'm a changed man. Just give me a chance to prove—"

She stands and walks back toward the elevator.

He follows her. "One chance. That's all I'm asking for. You came here in search of me, and now I'm here, giving myself to you."

She steps into the elevator and as the door closes she hears him say, "I'm not going to let you go like this. We can be happy together; I know we can. All I'm asking for is a chance to—"

TROUBLED MINDS

The walk back to the Hotel Baltimore is long, and to Andrew it seems even longer than it actually is. His thoughts are like a movie reel circling through his mind. There are images of their days together and of Max tilting her mouth to his, but they are intermingled with the picture of her looking into the face of Julien, the ex-lover. Early on Max said she'd come to Paris in search of this man. Now that she's found him, what next?

By the time Andrew reaches the Hotel Baltimore, both his brain and body are weary. He would like nothing better than to fall into bed and close his eyes, but sleep is impossible to come by. Closing his eyes only starts the movie all over again. There are no answers in the images, only questions.

MAX IS EXHAUSTED, AND HER head aches. It is nearly two-thirty and still she cannot sleep. The logical part of her heart argues that she should rid herself of Julien for good, but the old memories refuse to let go. He is like a shoe that pinches your foot.

Uncomfortable though it may be, you hang on to it because of its beauty.

Perhaps if she took an aspirin... As Max rummages through her bag in search of an aspirin, she sees the tea Annie gave her. Remembering the calming effect of the tea, she pulls the box from her bag. A cup or two might allow her to sleep.

At 2:30AM she pulls on jeans and a tee shirt and goes to the tiny breakfast room in back of the lobby. Come morning this room will be thick with the aroma of coffee and crowded with people, but now it is dark and empty. Running her hand along the wall, she feels for the light switch and snaps it on. Good, they have left the teakettle on the counter. She fills it with water and sets it on to boil.

Opening the box, she takes the infuser and fills it with the last of the mix. The kettle whistles, and she pours water into the cup. After the tea has turned a golden amber color, she sits at the table and sips it slowly.

It is sweet without sugar and as relaxing as she remembers. She curls her fingers around the warm cup and remembers Annie's words. There is no such thing as a love potion, but this will protect you from making a mistake.

Thinking back over all that has happened, Max remains there for a long time. When she finishes the first cup, she brews a second and carries it back to her room.

ANDREW WATCHES THE CLOCK TICK the minutes off. It is one-thirty, then two, but still he is thinking of Max. Surely by now she has decided something. Will it be to allow this ex-lover back into her life or turn away from him?

By 2:35AM the questions hammering at his brain are more

than he can stand. He picks up the telephone and calls Max's hotel.

The Vendome is a small hotel, and there is no night attendant. There is only a mechanical voice that says to dial the room number of the person you wish to speak with. This message is repeated first in French and then English. If you do not know the room number, it says, press one for the directory.

Andrew presses one; then, using the telephone keypad, he taps out the first four letters of Max's last name. The voice responds with "Maxine Martinelli, Room 3-1-7."

He clicks 3-1-7, and the telephone in Max's room rings. He waits. It rings nine times; then another voice comes on saying his party is not available and asking if he wants to leave a message.

Andrew doesn't. He hangs up; leaving a message is like watching another rerun of the reel in his head. It raises more questions but offers no answers.

He wonders if Max is still in the lobby. Is it possible they are talking things over? Perhaps this Julien has been searching for her just as she came searching for him. Andrew pictures the look of desperation he saw on Julien's face. He is certain a man with such a look wants something.

Andrew tries to imagine the possibilities. He came to catch up on old times? No, he looked too desperate. Borrow money? A possibility. Ask her to take him back? A very real possibility. In the past she belonged to him; did he come to reclaim her?

When the thoughts begin to grow heavy in his head Andrew goes to the minibar, opens it and removes a tiny bottle of scotch. He pours the amber liquid into a glass and takes a sip. For almost a half hour he paces the room; when he is too weary to continue pacing he sits on the side of the bed and tries to think.

His thoughts go back to Liza, and he remembers the pain of separation. This is not something he wants to go through again.

These memories of yesteryear argue that he should forget Max and move on, but he finds this impossible to do.

In the short time they have spent together he has felt happier than ever before. He tries to tell himself that, despite this, there is the possibility that it simply wasn't meant to be. But he doesn't believe it. Not for one minute.

WHEN SHE FINISHES THE SECOND cup of tea, Max yawns and leans back into her pillow. Minutes later she is sound asleep.

THE ROOM IS UNFAMILIAR, AND yet there are pieces of it that Max recognizes: the teacups from her mother's china, the parson's chairs pictured in her Someday portfolio, a scrap of fabric folded into a napkin. On the far wall a large window overlooks a stretch of grass. Scattered along the edges are bursts of color. Azaleas, hydrangeas, bluebells and a dogwood tree heavy with blossoms. She catches the scent of jasmine, and from somewhere close by she can hear the sound of children at play.

Annie sits across from her and holds a baby on her lap. She tickles the baby's tummy, and it giggles. These sounds are familiar, but from where Max cannot say.

"This is all so confusing," she says.

Annie smiles. "It's not that confusing; you'll get used to it."

Max studies the room, soaking up every small detail: the potted violet on the kitchen windowsill, the aged patina of the wainscoting, the sheer curtain drawn back with a single ribbon.

"It's seems I know this place," she says.

Annie laughs. "I should hope so. You designed it."

"But…" Max stutters, "how did I get here?"

Again Annie laughs. "You made the right choice."

"How? How could I make the right choice when I'm still so confused? Was it because of the magic in the tea?"

"There is no magic," Annie says. "The tea only calms you so you can see the truth of what's in your heart. The magic comes from loving someone."

"But—"

"It's late, and I've got to get home," Annie says. "Oliver will be—"

"This isn't your house?" Max asks.

Annie laughs again. "Of course not. Oliver and I are still at Memory House. We'll be there for the rest of our lives and then some." She stands, calls to the children playing in the yard and then hands the baby to Max.

As Annie shoos the two youngsters out the door she turns back. "Don't forget, we're expecting you and Andrew for dinner Sunday."

Max looks down at the baby in her arms and sees it has Andrew's soft gray eyes. A swell of love comes into her heart; it is so huge the force of it wakes her.

MAX

Last night when Julien said how much he needed me, I have to admit I was swayed. How could I not be? I've spent the last three years hoping and praying to hear just that. Wishing for something for so long and then turning away when you finally get it feels kind of weird. It's like climbing a mountain and then moments before you step onto the summit turning and going back down. Even if in your heart you know the top of the mountain is a volcano that will suck you in and destroy every dream you've ever had you still reach for it, because it's what you've been wanting for so long.

Don't worry; I'm not going to make the same mistake twice.

Spending this past week with Andrew has made me see what love should be. Love is supposed to be sweet and kind and thoughtful. Love shouldn't be endless days of heartache and feeling miserable. I wish I had realized this years ago; I'd have saved myself a whole lot of heartache.

I know Andrew likes me—a lot. I can't say for sure he loves me. I can't even say for sure I'm in love with him. It's too soon. But this afternoon we'll be flying home together, and once we get back to Virginia we'll have time to figure things out.

Hopefully.

When Andrew left last night he didn't even stop to look back. I *imagine he is pretty disappointed in me. Disappointed and maybe even hurt. He's a great guy and doesn't deserve that. I need to let Andrew see that I like him every bit as much as he likes me, and I think I know how to do it.*

The sun isn't even up yet and I've had less than four hours sleep, but I really don't care. I'm going to jump in the shower, get dressed and hurry over to the Hotel Baltimore. I'll go straight to Andrew's room, and when he opens the door I'll wrap my arms around him and kiss him smack on the mouth. That ought to show him exactly how I feel. Afterward I'll suggest we go to breakfast together. That's when I'll tell him Julien is ancient history. I can already see the smile Andrew is going to have when he hears me say that.

I'm not going to mention the dream. It's too soon, and besides it really was only a dream. Wasn't it?

MISSED CONNECTIONS

It is a long while before Andrew finally falls asleep. He dozes for less than two hours then is awake again. It is almost six o'clock; surely she is back in the room by now. He again calls the Hotel Vendome, and when the mechanical voice answers he taps in 3-1-7. The telephone rings nine times; then the recording answers.

Andrew slams the phone down. "Dammit!" He stomps back and forth across the room several times then decides.

It takes him less than ten minutes to pack; then he storms out of the room. He is a fool to care. A fool to let a week's worth of fun morph into something more than what it is. He stops at the desk, checks out, then leaves the hotel and climbs into a taxicab.

"Charles de Gaulle airport," he says.

MAX TURNS OFF THE SHOWER and listens. A moment ago she thought she heard the telephone. Wrapping a towel around herself and leaving a trail of drips across the bathroom tile, she hurries in and lifts the receiver. A dial tone, that's it. The message light is not flashing, but still she taps 4 and waits.

224

"You have no messages," the recording says.

"That's odd," she mumbles then returns to the bathroom.

Twenty minutes later she is dressed and ready to go, but still she is thinking of the telephone call. On the off chance that it was Andrew, she picks up the telephone and calls the Hotel Baltimore. It will spoil the surprise of her standing right there in front of him, but better that than to have him call and think she is avoiding his call.

"Hotel Baltimore," the clerk answers.

"May I speak with Andrew Steen?" Max asks.

For a moment there is nothing; then the clerk says, "Mister Steen has already checked out."

Max's heart drops into her stomach.

WHEN THE TAXICAB PULLS AWAY from the curb Andrew leans back in the seat. If Max wants to be with Julien then so be it, he tells himself. A voice in the back of his head asks, *Seriously?*

"Yes, seriously," he says aloud.

"Pardon?" the taxi driver replies.

"Oh, it was nothing," Andrew says. "I was just thinking out loud." He hesitates then adds, "Trying to make a decision." He discounts the fact that ten minutes earlier he'd already done so.

ALTHOUGH HE'S DECIDED TO GO home and forget about her, Andrew is still thinking about Max. The truth is he really likes her. Loves her maybe. *Isn't something like that worth fighting for?* the voice asks.

Andrew thinks back to the first case he ever argued in a courtroom. Everyone said it was a case that was all but impossible to win, and yet he'd won it. He'd believed in Tom Crystal's innocence, and he'd fought for it tooth and nail. He runs the movie reel through his mind again, picturing the way Max looped her arm through his as they walked side by side, the way her body fit so perfectly into his when they slept together, the way she lifted her face to his and offered a kiss. He didn't just take it; she gave it.

Yeah, a relationship like this is *worth fighting for.*

He taps the driver on the shoulder. "I've changed my mind. Take me to the Hotel Vendome."

AFTER MAX HANGS UP THE telephone, she brushes back a tear then pulls her suitcase from the closet and hurriedly begins to pack. Last night it was after midnight when Andrew turned his back and walked away. The first flight going to anywhere in America doesn't leave until seven-thirty, which means he might still be at the airport.

As she slams the suitcase shut, the telephone rings. Leaping across the bed she grabs the receiver and says, "Andrew?"

"No," the caller answers icily. "It's Julien."

"Oh." The disappointment in her voice is obvious.

He ignores it. "I meant what I said last night. I hope you can find it in your heart to forgive a foolish man who—"

"Enough," she cuts in. "You are who you are, Julien. No one is ever going to change you, and I have no interest in trying. We were wrong from the start—"

"Maxine, wait!" The timbre of his voice changes; it becomes arrogant and commanding. "You're making a mistake. A big mistake!"

"My only mistake would be letting you back into my life."

When she hangs up, it is as if a huge boulder has been lifted from her shoulders. She shrugs on her jacket and heads for the elevator. As she waits she hears the telephone start to ring again, but when the doors whoosh open, she steps in and pushes "Lobby".

THE VENDOME IS A SMALL hotel on a side street. It is not a place where taxicabs park and wait for passengers to happen by. When Max stops at the desk to check out, she asks the clerk to call for a taxi.

"I'm in a hurry," she says, "so ask if they can get here as soon as possible."

He makes the call then says, "Five minutes or less."

Max gives an appreciative nod. "I'll wait out front." She takes her bag and walks outside.

It is early and there is very little traffic. It is less than a minute until Max sees the taxi speeding down Rue d'Arris. She glances at her watch: 6:45. It is going to be close, very close, but hopefully she'll make it. When the taxi comes to a stop in front of the hotel, she already has her suitcase in hand.

She reaches for the door, but it pops open before she touches the handle. A long leg steps out just as she bends to get in. She gasps.

"Andrew?"

Without giving her a chance to say anything more, he pulls her into his arms and presses her to his chest. He leans down, his cheek touching hers, the sweet sound of his breath in her ear.

"Any man dumb enough to let you get away the first time doesn't deserve a second chance," he says.

She lifts her face to his, and he kisses her full on the mouth. It is a kiss such as Max has never before known. It is both tender and passionate. It is filled with the warm memories of what they have shared for the past six days, and it is also a promise of all that is to come.

GOING HOME

"Do you want me to wait?" the taxi driver asks.

"Yes," Andrew answers; then he turns to Max. "I came here looking for you," he says softly. "Where were you going?"

She smiles. "To try and find you. When I called your hotel they said you'd already checked out, so I thought I might be able to catch you at the airport."

"I called you too," Andrew says. "Twice. When there was no answer I thought you'd gone off with—"

"Why didn't you leave a message?"

Andrew gives a sheepish grin. "It was two-thirty in the morning. I figured you were still with him, and that ticked me off."

"I wasn't," Max says. "I was in the breakfast room having a cup of tea."

"Tea? At two-thirty in the morning?"

"It's a long story," Max says. "Someday I'll tell you all about it."

When Andrew folds Max into his arms for a second time, the taxi driver gives his horn a short blast.

"The meter's still running," he says. "You want me to keep waiting?"

"We're through waiting," Andrew replies. "We're going to the airport. Pop the trunk, and I'll put the lady's suitcase in."

AFTER THE BAGS ARE CHECKED, Andrew goes to the service desk and upgrades both tickets to first class. He smiles and tells the attendant at the desk they are celebrating. What he doesn't say.

The Air France clerk watches them walk away, his arm curled around her waist, her head tilted toward his shoulder. She picks up the gray phone and buzzes the boarding gate agent.

"I think you've got a pair of newlyweds on board," she says. "Seats Six A and B."

IT IS THREE HOURS UNTIL flight time so they go to breakfast and talk, partly about the future and partly of the past. Max tells him she no longer has any feelings for Julien.

"What the heart remembers isn't always a true picture of what was," she says. "I doubt I ever really loved Julien; I was simply in love with the thought of love." She hesitates then gives an easy smile. "It was Paris. He was a free-spirited artist rebelling against society, and I was a very impressionable young architect."

Andrew stretches his arm across the table and takes her hand in his.

"What about now?" he says. It is a question about both past and present.

"Well, I'm still an architect," she says laughingly; then her words take on a more serious tone. "But I've learned love isn't the flourishes and fancy ironwork that decorate a facade, it's the foundation of a building. It's what forever is built on."

Andrew squeezes her hand affectionately. "I've heard lawyers make a very good cornerstone."

She gives him a smile. "Funny, I've heard that very same thing."

MAX SUSPECTS THE DREAM WAS more than just a dream. She believes the tea enabled her to peek into their future, but she says nothing. There is plenty of time. Some rainy evening when the baby is sleeping and they are snuggled in front of the fireplace, she will tell him of the dream. He will laugh and claim it is her vivid imagination just as Oliver does with Annie. Like Oliver he will say there is no such thing as a magic tea, but Max knows better.

IT HAS BEEN A NIGHT of worry and sleeplessness so despite the three cups of coffee they've downed, they are both yawning when the loudspeaker crackles that Air France Flight 687 is now loading at Gate B11. They pull themselves out of the booth and head down the long corridor that leads to the gates, walking slowly and leaning into one another as if this is a prediction of the years to come.

Once they are seated on the plane, the stewardess brings them glasses of champagne. After only a few sips Max and Andrew are both sound asleep. He has his legs stretched out and his head laid back; she is cuddled next to him, her head resting on his chest.

The next time Max opens her eyes, Flight 687 is crossing Nova Scotia. She taps Andrew's arm and he wakes. "Do you have your car at the airport?"

He gives a sleepy nod.

"Annie was going to meet me; should I call her and say don't bother?"

Another nod. "Tell her we'll meet them at their house, but don't explain."

Max laughs. She loves the thought of such a surprise. She calls Annie from the plane.

"Don't come to the airport," she says. "We'll stop by your house."

Annie hears the happiness in Max's voice, and she likes the sound of the word "we"; obviously Ophelia was right. Max is coming home happy and in love.

"You two better plan on staying for dinner," she says.

Max looks across at Andrew. "Dinner?"

He gives a grin and nods his approval.

WHEN ANNIE HANGS UP THE telephone, she turns to Oliver and says, "Max is coming for dinner, and she's with Julien!"

Oliver raises a skeptical eyebrow. "Did she say that?"

"Well, she didn't specifically say Julien, but who else would it be?"

Oliver shrugs and turns back to his newspaper.

Annie, too excited to contain herself, calls Ophelia.

"You were right," she says. "Max is coming home with Julien."

"Julien? The French lad?" Ophelia sounds a bit puzzled.

"Yes," Annie answers, "and she's as happy as you thought she'd be."

"That's odd," Ophelia muses. "You're sure he's the one with her?"

"Yes. She called from the plane and said they'd come for dinner."

Again Ophelia questions that it's Julien, and again Annie says she is almost positive of it.

"Strange," Ophelia says. "That's not the way I saw it."

"But you said—"

"I knew Max would come home happy and in love, but I didn't figure it to be the French lad. Did you give her the special traveler's tea?"

"Of course. I put it in a box with the silver infuser just as you said."

"Maybe she didn't use it," Ophelia replies. In her mind, this is the only logical explanation for things going awry.

By the time they hang up, Annie is beginning to have her doubts. Ophelia is almost never wrong. She has an uncanny ability to know what will happen and who it will happen to. And yet…

THREE HOURS LATER ANNIE HEARS the car pull into the driveway. She runs to the door, and as she steps out onto the front porch Andrew climbs from the car. Seconds later Max steps out of the other side.

For a moment Annie just stands there, dumbfounded.

"Aren't you going to welcome us home?" Max asks with a huge grin.

"Us?" Annie replies. "You and Andrew?"

They both nod happily.

That evening over dinner Max tells the story of all that happened. She leaves out the fact that Julien was one of the thieves. It is still too shameful a story to share. Someday she will tell Annie and Andrew both, but not now. Not when there is so much happiness to be celebrated.

It is almost eleven when Max and Andrew stand to leave. As Max hugs Annie to her chest she whispers, "Last year when you invited Andrew and me to the dinner party it was supposed to be a fix-up, wasn't it?"

Holding back a smug grin, Annie replies, "Why on earth would you think a thing like that?"

OPHELIA

W ell, I guess by now you know everything happened as I said it would. Max went through a rough time but came home happy and very much in love. I'll admit, I was a tad surprised when Annie first told me she was with the French fellow. I've never known traveler's tea to fail, but Max is a spitfire and nearly as unpredictable as that storm so I wasn't sure she'd used it. Overcoming unrealistic expectations is almost impossible without some sort of help, but that's something people need to find out for themselves.

Now that the situation has come full circle, I should confess to one small fib: traveler's tea is actually the tea of truth. It's not magic, but it sharpens a person's mind so that they can see the truth of the situation they're in. It works quite well for affairs of the heart, but it's not terribly effective in financial matters.

I seldom use this tea, because truth is something most people would rather not know about. They go through life with a boatload of pie-in-the-sky expectations, and truth simply gets in the way.

Like everyone else, I've got my own expectations and perhaps that's a good thing. It gives me something to pray about. The night of the storm I half-expected Edward to come for me, but I asked the Lord to wait a while. I said before leaving this earth, I wanted to experience the joy of being a grandma.

The blessed event happened, but not exactly as I thought it would. In late May Annie did have a beautiful little girl with eyes as violet as her own, but she also had a boy. Twins. The boy they named Ethan after Oliver's daddy. Annie said she was going to name the girl Ophelia after me, and I told her, Don't you dare! Ophelia is no name for a sweet little baby.

Two days later they named the child Starr. I like to think Annie picked that name because of my Edward. She knows I find him up there in the stars. One day he'll come for me, I know that, but until then I'm just going to enjoy being a grandma and watching these little ones grow up. I won't be here for the whole of their life but I've peeked into the future, and I can tell you the boy will be true to his namesake and the girl will have powers way past Annie's or mine. Her touch will cause a wilted flower to bloom again and an angry animal to grow calm. But all that's in the future; years after Edward and I have been reunited.

THIS MORNING THE BABIES WERE christened, and afterward there was a party at Memory House. Every living soul in Burnsville was there, and Baylor Towers had to hire an extra car to cart the lot of us over and back.

Max and Andrew are godparents for both babies. A good choice, I must say. Seeing how they fussed over those babies, I bet it won't be too long before they start a family of their own. Max is already wearing a diamond engagement ring, and she's drawing up plans for a house that she says came to her in a dream.

On the ride home I told Lillian it was good to see Memory House alive and bustling again. People with love to share are what give the place its special magic.

God knows I searched long and hard before Annie happened along, but the first time I laid eyes on her I suspected she was the one. I was right. She's brought new life to the house in more ways than I could have *ever imagined. This summer the garden is chock full of herbs and spices, and there are flowers every color of the rainbow. The apothecary has never been busier. Now customers are in and out of the shop all day long.*

At the party Ida Tallmadge said her daughter Cynthia was at long last engaged, thanks to Annie's tonic. And Elmer Grimes claims his gout is cured—completely and utterly cured.

I also saw Cheryl Ann Ferguson looking at those babies of Annie's, and I knew exactly what she was thinking. It happens every year at just about the same time. My heart aches for the poor girl, but there's nothing anyone can do. What's done is done, and there's no turning back.

I still remember that awful year and all the heartache Cheryl Ann went through. Back then she was barely nineteen and faced with the most painful decision of her life. She did what she had to do, but the memory of it still haunts her.

This year will be the worst one ever. Before the winter is out, she'll come into the apothecary asking for Annie's help. But Cheryl Ann's story is another tale, and I can't go into it right now. You'll learn the details soon enough...

FROM THE AUTHOR

If you enjoyed reading this book, please post a review at your favorite on-line retailer and share your thoughts with other readers.

I'd love to hear from you. If you visit my website and sign up to receive my monthly newsletter, as a special thank you, you'll receive a copy of
A HOME IN HOPEFUL

http://betteleecrosby.com

What the Heart Remembers is Book Three in the Memory House Series.

Turn the page to peek inside the other Memory House Books.

MEMORY HOUSE

Book One, The Memory House Series

Annie Cross is running from a broken love affair when she stops at the tiny bed and breakfast inn. She is looking to forget the past, but what she finds is a future filled with the magic of lost memories. A heartwarming story of love and friendship. Winner of the Reader's Favorite Southern Fiction Silver Medal.

THE LOFT

Book Two, The Memory House Series

Fifty years of memories are hidden in the walls of the loft. Now Ophelia Browne is leaving the house and she's leaving some very powerful memories behind. Annie needs to find just one...the one that will save Oliver's life. A story of believing in miracles and the power of love.

SPARE CHANGE

Book One, The Wyattsville Series

Winner of five Literary Awards, *Spare Change* has been compared to John Grisham's *The Client*. Eleven-year-old Ethan Allen Doyle has witnessed a brutal murder and now the boy is running for his life. Olivia Westerly is the only person he can trust, and he's not too sure he can trust her. She's got no love of children and a truckload of superstitions—one of them is the belief that eleven is the unluckiest number on earth.

JUBILEE'S JOURNEY
Book Two, The Wyattsville Series

Winner of the 2014 FPA President's Book Award Gold Medal, *Jubilee's Journey* is the story of a child born in the West Virginia mountains and orphaned before she is seven. When she and her older brother go in search of an aunt, he is caught up in a crime not of his making. Jubilee knows the truth, but who is going to believe a seven-year-old child?

PASSING THROUGH PERFECT
Book Three, The Wyattsville Series

Passing through Perfect is a story rife with the injustices of the South and rich with the compassion of strangers. It's 1946. The war is over. Millions of American soldiers are coming home and Benjamin Church is one of them. After four years of being away he thought things in Alabama would have changed, but they haven't. Grinder's Corner is as it's always been—a hardscrabble burp in the road. It's not much, but it's home.

THE TWELFTH CHILD
Book One, The Serendipity Series

The Twelfth Child is an uplifting tale of trust, love and friendship. To escape a planned marriage, a willful daughter leaves home and makes her way in a Depression-era world. When she is nearing the tail end of her years, she meets the young woman with whom she forges a friendship that lasts beyond life.

PREVIOUSLY LOVED TREASURES
Book Two, The Serendipity Series

Previously Loved Treasures is a story that resonates with heartwarming albeit quirky characters and the joy of a pay-it-forward philosophy. When Ida Sweetwater opens a rooming house, she will find the granddaughter she never knew she had and turn a group of haphazard strangers into a family.

WISHING FOR WONDERFUL
The Serendipity Series, Book Three

Wishing for Wonderful is a story narrated by a Cupid with attitude. It will have you laughing out loud as Cupid uses a homeless dog in his scheme to give two deserving couples the love they deserve.

More Great Reading

CRACKS IN THE SIDEWALK

A *USA Today* Bestseller and Winner of the 2014 Reader's Favorite Gold Medal, *Cracks in the Sidewalk* is a powerful family saga that is a heartrending reminder of how fragile relationships can be. Based on the true story of a woman's search for her missing grandchildren.

WHAT MATTERS MOST

In *What Matters Most* Louise Palmer is faced with life-altering changes and must choose between friendships and marriage. Although it is at times laugh-out-loud funny, beneath the humor there is a message of love, tolerance and coming to grips with reality.

BLUEBERRY HILL

Blueberry Hill asks the poignant question—can love save a person from self-destruction? In a heartrending memoir Crosby looks back to a time when the sisters were young enough to feel invincible and foolish enough to believe it would last forever.

ABOUT THE AUTHOR

AWARD-WINNING NOVELIST BETTE LEE CROSBY brings the wit and wisdom of her Southern Mama to works of fiction—the result is a delightful blend of humor, mystery and romance.

"Storytelling is in my blood," Crosby laughingly admits, "My mom was not a writer, but she was a captivating storyteller, so I find myself using bits and pieces of her voice in most everything I write."

Crosby's work was first recognized in 2006 when she received The National League of American Pen Women Award for a then unpublished manuscript. Since then, she has gone on to win numerous other awards, including The Reviewer's Choice Award, The Reader's Favorite Gold Medal, FPA President's Book Award Gold Medal and The Royal Palm Literary Award.

To learn more about Bette Lee Crosby, explore her other work, or read a sample from any of her books, visit her blog at:

http://betteleecrosby.com